"I've receive admitted.

"From the Hors Verbal? Electro

"What difference does it make?" He pegged me with a look that set my heart galloping with panic and...something else.

"You know, it could give us a clue."

"Us?"

Ross Hardel had a bad habit of driving me to exasperation. And, I realised, I'd almost blown my cover. "Yes, us. Me, you, everybody who works at the stable. My job as your groom is to keep your horse safe."

He grunted. "If I didn't know better, I'd think you were an undercover cop—or something."

Available in November 2006 from Silhouette Sensation

Awaken to Danger
by Catherine Mann
(Wingmen Warriors)

Living on the Edge
by Susan Mallery

Breaking All the Rules
by Susan Vaughan

Look-Alike
by Meredith Fletcher
(Bombshell)

Blue Jeans and a Badge
by Nina Bruhns

Ms Longshot
by Sylvie Kurtz
(Bombshell)

Ms Longshot

SYLVIE KURTZ

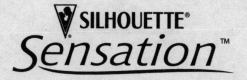

SILHOUETTE®
Sensation™

Silhouette, Silhouette Sensation and Colophon are registered
trademarks of Harlequin Books S.A., used under licence.

First published in Great Britain 2006
Silhouette Books, Eton House, 18-24 Paradise Road,
Richmond, Surrey TW9 1SR

© Harlequin Books S.A. 2005

Special thanks and acknowledgement are given to Sylvie Kurtz for
her contribution to THE IT GIRLS series.

ISBN-13: 978 0 373 51384 0
ISBN-10: 0 373 51384 4

18-1106

Printed and bound in Spain
by Litografía Rosés S.A., Barcelona

SYLVIE KURTZ

Flying an eight-hour solo cross-country in a Piper Arrow with only the aeroplane's crackling radio and a large bag of M&M's for company, Sylvie Kurtz realised a pilot's life wasn't for her. The stories zooming in and out of her mind proved more entertaining than the flight itself. Not a quitter, she finished her pilot's course and earned her commercial licence and instrument rating.

Since then, she has traded in her wings for a keyboard, where she lets her imagination soar to create fictional adventures that explore the power of love and the thrill of suspense. When not writing, she enjoys the outdoors with her husband and two children, quilt-making, photography and reading whatever catches her interest.

You can write to Sylvie at PO Box 702, Milford, NH 03055, USA. And visit her website at www.sylviekurtz.com.

For Cassie—a Bombshell in training ☺

A special thank-you:
To Amy Schiff for sharing her story with me.
Definitely a Bombshell heroine!
Samantha at Hair Force for helping
me with my dyeing dilemma.
Ann Voss Peterson for sharing
horse trailer stories.

Prologue

New York City. December. Ten years ago.

The second-floor bathroom of the Constance Gramercy School for Girls was crowded as usual. I elbowed my way to the mirror and puckered up to see if the zit I'd felt growing on my chin in social science had popped up. Wouldn't you know it, the timing sucked. I had a horse show in the morning.

Nathalie Huston, my best friend since we'd bitten each other the first day of kindergarten, came pounding through the door, big boobs leading the way and her long, black ponytail flying behind her. She'd had that magnificent chest since she was eleven. At fifteen, I was still waiting for mine to show up. My mother said British roses took longer to bloom, which only made me wish I'd inherited more of my father's American genes.

Back of the hand pressed to her forehead, Nat paused and sighed dramatically. Of course the contrast of Wedgwood-blue eyes and raven hair had made her dramatic from birth. I couldn't help smiling.

"What's wrong this time, Nat?" I turned back to the mirror and swiped boring clear lipgloss—the only kind the builds-the-character rules allowed— across my lips.

"Oh, Alexa, I can't take it anymore." Nat plopped her book bag against the white sink and checked to see if what little makeup was allowed needed retouching. "I simply can't sit through Mr. Ziegler's algebra class today." She sniffed in perfect imitation of Mr. Ziegler's postnasal drip problem and pushed nonexistent glasses up her nose—just as Mr. Ziegler would do. "Forty minutes of *that* is enough to drive anyone nuts. Like what am I ever going to use algebra for anyway?"

I didn't mind math. I was kind of good at it, actually. Daddy kept telling me I had a head for business and, as uncool as that was, I liked hearing him say it.

"Let's cut last period," Nat whispered. She stretched open the top of her Gucci bag and showed off the fresh pack of smokes.

"It's raining," I said with a sigh. No need to look

outside for a weather update. Not with the frizz I had going. Even in a French braid, even inside, even with half a bottle of Aveda frizz tamer, the humidity made my mahogany curls look like one of the rusted Brillo pads in the science lab.

"I've got an umbrella." Nat grinned and tugged on the minicompact, red-plaid Burberry umbrella tucked in her bag.

I made a quick calculation. With two weeks left to the semester before the Christmas break, I could afford another warning on my record before someone notified my parents they had a delinquent daughter. Besides, Daddy had promised to pick me up right after school today so we could get to the Ridgefield Winter Dressage Show early. If I was already standing outside, he wouldn't have to wait for me.

I slung my Coach bag over my shoulder. "I'm in. Let's go."

Traffic honked up and down Ninety-third Street. Breathing in that exhaust had to fry our lungs more than any cigarette could. Nat popped open the umbrella and passed it to me. I angled it to shield us from most of the rain. Cold wind pried apart the blue cashmere Marc Jacobs coat I'd pulled from my bag, but I didn't care. I hated stuffy English almost as much as Nat hated algebra. Shivering outside was a small price to pay to miss the dreaded class.

I untucked my boring white Calvin Klein buttondown shirt, rolled the waist of my gray uniform skirt and leaned back against the cold stone wall. What was the point of having great legs if you couldn't show them off? And what idiot had come up with gray as the uniform color in the first place? No one I knew looked good in gray.

Nat passed a coffin stick. "I can't wait for break."

I lit it with the gold lighter I'd pilfered from my mother's purse and puffed out a geyser of smoke. "Me either."

"Sucks that I'll be stuck going skiing with my dad in Aspen again, though." Nat made a face. "He's bringing his new girlfriend." A gold-digging bimbo only seven years older than Nat.

"Maybe you'll get lucky and she'll run into a tree," I sympathized.

"She's more into the *après* than the ski, if you know what I mean." Nat took a long drag on her cigarette. "What are you going to wear to the Black-and-White Ball?"

"Ralph sent over a black number that's so hot," I said, practically purring. My long legs had caught Ralph Lauren's attention when I was thirteen, and he'd tried to get me to pose for one of his ads ever since. Naturally my mother had nixed the idea. Modeling is apparently beneath the station of Lady Cheltingham's daughter. I secretly believed that my stiff-upper-lip mother just didn't want me to have any kind of fun. Still, for every major event, a dress appeared at our Park Avenue penthouse, and even my mother wasn't too proud to accept the gift of couture.

"It's cut down to here." I twisted my body around without moving my feet and dragged a hand down to the small of my back.

At that moment, someone leaned on a horn and didn't let go. Tires screeched and a yellow taxi hopped the curb, trying to avoid a collision with a town car zigzagging like crazy through traffic.

He's not going to stop, I realized as the taxi charged toward us.

The world slowed around me as I untwisted my feet. My heart pounded a ragged beat against my eardrums. A gust of wind wrenched the umbrella from my hand. Nat's screams echoed as if she were in a tunnel. Too late, I lifted a leg to bolt out of the way. The thud of metal against stone and bone registered as something foreign and far away—like it was all happening to someone else—pinning me to the wall like a butterfly.

The taxi recoiled. I fell and I could tell you every second of the trip to the pavement. Inanely what floated through my mind was Newton's First Law I'd learned in Mrs. Collin's science class: "For every action there's an equal and opposite reaction." And the weirdest thing of all was the way my head bounced sideways against the wet concrete like a tennis ball, splashing dirty puddle water into my eyes. When my vision cleared, what filled my sight was the perfectly whole cigarette, end glowing red, between my fingers.

Well, crap, I thought as pain screamed through my body and pierced my brain. Daddy was right. Cigarettes *were* going to kill me.

Chapter 1

New York City Late April. Present.

I was probably the only undercover agent in history who'd get fired for removing her prosthesis in an airport and pissing off a French gendarme. But the hyper frog barking at me in French at the security checkpoint at Charles de Gaulle had far exceeded my limit of patience when he refused to understand that my leg was setting off the alarm, not a hidden weapon.

Ever since the accident, I'd been sensitive about my leg. So when my cell phone rang shortly after my flight touched down in New York and I was sum-

moned to tea at the Gotham Rose Club, I was sure
the ax was about to fall and I was going to get booted
out of their secret agency.

The car service dropped me off in front of the
gray cut-stone townhouse that housed the Gotham
Rose Club on Sixty-eighth Street between Park and
Madison on the Upper East Side. I stood outside the
black wrought-iron security grate over the carved
wood front door with its rose design and pretended
to admire the architecture. Mostly I was composing
myself.

Renee Dalton-Sinclair ran the Gotham Rose Club,
an elite, members-only club intended to attract
young, wealthy New York women like me to fund-
raise and volunteer their time for charity. I was doing both for the Horses of Hope Foundation long
before Renee asked me to join. But Renee also had
another use for the club—taking down high-society
criminals. And that's why I was here today, and why
I couldn't decide if the nerves jumping around like
fleas on a barn dog were from anger or anxiety.

I tugged at the hem of the silver-leaf sleeveless V-
neck top and smoothed the ivory Vera Wang cotton-
tulle skirt with my sweaty palms, then pressed the
doorbell. Olivia Hayworth's voice sang across the in-
tercom. "Welcome, Alexa. Come on in."

A security buzzer released the latch and I walked
into a white Italian marble foyer that reminded me
of a gilded cage. The place smelled of old money and

older traditions. And despite my background, I never felt like I quite fit in.

Olivia, Renee's assistant, greeted me with an extended hand and a bright smile that eased some of my anxiety. Okay, so maybe I'd just get a warning.

"Hello, Alexa, how was your trip to Paris?"

"Nonstop crazy."

Olivia chuckled. "With Nathalie Huston, what else did you expect?"

I winced. Maybe this *was* about the incident with the gendarme.

My silver Delman ballet flats echoed against the marble as Olivia led me back to the Irish tearoom, one of the many that served as meeting rooms. Renee sat alone at the table. That couldn't be good. My stomach took a sharp dive south.

Renee's hair was pulled into a French twist. The hint of gray snaking through her auburn locks here and there merely added to the air of dignity that surrounded her. The winter white of her Chanel suit complemented her creamy complexion. As always, her smile was warm and welcoming and her striking royal blue eyes assessing.

The reason I'd joined Renee's secret agency was to prove to myself that I *could* do anything I wanted—even catch bad guys. Not to mention the promise of excitement—which, I should mention, had failed to materialize. Unless you counted poring through piles of business reports as exciting—which

I did not. For some reason, Renee insisted on treating me as if I were Swarovski crystal.

Frankly, I don't know why Renee asked me to join the Gotham Rose Club when she barely made use of my skills. My guess was that it was some sort of employer requirement—round out the roll call with a token cripple and get patted on the head for following all the equal-employment opportunity rules. She knew how I felt, and that didn't make me one of her favorite agents.

I often thought that the illusive Governess was the one who'd insisted Renee hire me, and Renee had done so only reluctantly. Of course, who the Governess was and what she had at stake in this cloak-and-dagger agency was as mysterious as why Renee had agreed to play front woman for the agency. I had to admit curiosity was one of the things that kept me coming back.

Renee pushed away a file and rose. A small smile lifted the corners of her lips. "Come in, Alexa. Sit. Tea?"

A file was a good sign, right? Unless it contained a list of my transgressions.

I greeted Renee with a stiff air kiss. A vintage linen tablecloth covered the round Charles X table set with Hewitt Gold bone china and Pelham Gold flatware. Scones from my favorite bakery on Madison crammed a three-tiered silver Tiffany tray. Steam curled from the blue-and-white Lynn Feld porcelain teapot. White tea roses in a Lalique vase spiced the air. Renee had impeccable taste and it served as a perfect veil for the true work she did here. Still, I couldn't help wanting to throw a Tupperware tub on the table at one of the functions just to hear the proper ladies gasp.

"I'd love a cup of tea." I took the chair across from Renee's. Fragrant bergamot scented the air as Renee poured hot Earl Grey tea with slow precision into pale-blue, gold-trimmed cups.

"Where is everyone else?" I asked. Tea with Renee usually meant dealing with Tatiana Guttmann, Becca Whitmore and one or two more of the agents. I didn't have anything against them personally, but they got all the good assignments.

"It's just the two of us today." Renee slanted me another one of her cryptic smiles as she served me a cup.

"Oh." I forced my fingers to relax against the china. Was she going to fire me before I ever got any of that promised excitement? I tried to delay the inevitable. "How is Emma doing?"

Emma Bromwell, another agent who'd gone through the same training class I had, suffered a severe arm fracture and a concussion during an explosion at a post-Oscar fund-raising party for the Miller Children's Home in California a couple months ago.

Renee glanced away. A certain sadness seemed to weigh on her soul. I figured the sadness existed because her husband, Preston, whom she dearly loved, was serving prison time for fraud. Five years ago the case made headlines in all the papers. But asking about Emma seemed to carve deeper grooves into that sadness, aging her. Was she taking Emma's accident personally? Was this sense of personal responsibility why Renee never gave me a real assignment?

"Emma's doing as well as can be expected," Renee said. "She'll have to have physical therapy for a bit longer, but she'll regain full use of her arm."

"That's good." When I noticed my hand unconsciously rubbing at the edge of my socket, I snapped it back to the warmth of the teacup. "She was worried she wouldn't be able to play the piano anymore. And that brought her such joy." I knew how I'd felt when I'd thought I'd never ride again.

"How are the preparations for the Horses of Hope Foundation wine-and-cheese party going?" Renee asked.

"Fine." I placed my cup back on its saucer. "Tickets are selling well and sponsors are lining up to host a table, including the esteemed mayor of our city, Mr. Siegel."

"Can your assistant handle the rest of the preparations?"

Ah, so that was it. An assignment, not an indictment on my lack of propriety at Charles de Gaulle. My shoulders sagged with relief. "Yes, of course she can."

"Good." Renee added a slice of lemon to her

tea. "The Governess has asked me to send you on an assignment. I'll take over your hostessing duties at the show."

Send? As in field? I sat up a little straighter, and anticipation shot through my veins. Thank you, Governess! At least *someone* had faith in me.

None of the agents had ever met the mysterious Governess, not even Renee. The only thing we could agree on was that, whoever she was, she was well connected. And when the equally mysterious Duke entered the conversation, you'd think we were a book club discussing an old Victoria Holt novel.

The Duke was said to be some sort of Godfather-like figure who ran in elite circles and had fingers in all sorts of dirty dealings. If you believed the rumors, he had a hand in everything from corruption to gambling. I had a suspicion he was one of the reasons the Gotham Rose Club was started. But if Renee knew who he was, she wasn't spilling the secret.

It was all supposed to be hush-hush, but I'd heard that Renee had struck a deal with the Governess to create and run the Gotham Rose Agency in exchange for her husband, Preston's, early release from prison. Someone had to go to jail for the Sinclair family's illegal business dealings and poor Preston was the scapegoat.

"Have you been keeping up with the news of the show circuit?" Renee asked, reaching for a scone.

"No, not really." What was the point of salting a

wound? I got my fix of horses through my foundation and my weekly trips to my estate in Darien, Connecticut, where I kept two horses. "Why?"

"A string of accidents have happened this winter on the Palm Beach show-jumping circuit. Canterbury Crown died of a heart attack while going over a jump and his rider was hurt from the fall. Drug testing showed cocaine in the horse's blood."

"Cocaine?" Who would do such a thing? Of course, some people would do anything to win— even hurt a defenseless animal. "What happened?"

"The police investigated but came to no conclusion."

I leaned forward, my heart fluttering against my ribs. "You want me to look into it," I said hopefully.

"A few weeks later, a barn fire killed four horses, including the current National Horse Show champion, Total Eclipse."

Just thinking about the terror those poor animals had to endure raised my blood pressure and sparked my anger. But I bit my tongue. This was definitely my kind of assignment, but Renee was obviously not asking for my opinion.

"The latest victim is Monica Lightbourne, daughter of the media heiress," Renee continued. "Someone injected her horse, Blue Ribbon Belle, with a drug that caused a neurological reaction so violent the horse had to be put down."

"That's awful. How do you want me to help?"

"The Metropolitan Spring Classic Charity Horse Show begins in a week."

"You want me to investigate at the show since I'll be there for my foundation's charity event." Yes! This I could do. No stretch at all.

"Not exactly." Renee sipped her tea, humor glinting in her eyes. "As you know, the mayor's daughter participates in show jumping. Elliot Siegel is afraid his daughter, who's a front runner to win the Grand Prix, will be the Horse Ripper's next victim and that he'll strike some time before or during the show."

"You want me to protect Leah Siegel." A small thrill spurred my pulse into a gallop. Finally a chance to do more than shuffle paper. Protecting the mayor's daughter was an elite assignment.

"We want you to go undercover at the stable where she trains." Renee tilted her head. "As a groom."

"Excuse me?" I had to have heard wrong. Renee wanted *me* to go undercover as a *groom*? Just what had she put in her tea?

"You heard me."

Needing to gather my wits, I picked up my teacup, but it never made it to my lips. I plunked the cup back on its saucer. "You want me to shovel manure? How's that going to help protect Leah?"

Renee studied me, then lifted both eyebrows and a shoulder in a gesture of dismissal. "I told the Governess this wasn't a good idea. With your leg, you can't possibly be expected to perform such hard physical labor."

"Wait a minute. This has nothing to do with my leg." I slid to the edge of the chair caught between wanting to tell Renee what she could do with her condescending attitude and fighting for my first real assignment. I hadn't realized how badly I needed her approval until now. "You don't want me here. You never have."

"That's not true. The trouble with you, Alexa, is that you have no concept of the limits of your skills and that makes you dangerous. You think you can do everything. Everyone needs help. And I don't want to see you, or any of my girls, hurt."

Hurt? She was thinking of Emma. But the situations were different. Renee hadn't even given me the chance to chip a nail. The last assignment had relied more on my understanding of avionics and electronics systems produced by my father's defense-contracting business than on physical prowess.

I rode again after the doctors told me I never would. I survived the brutal training I'd gone through with Emma, Chloe and Becca. I ran the business side of my foundation without anyone there knowing about my handicap. My chin crept up and my back got stiff with steel. "I can do anything as well as anyone else."

The tilt of Renee's smile widened. "You're proving my point."

I strangled the linen napkin in one fist. *Control, Alexa. Get yourself under control.* If I didn't watch out, I'd blow this. I had to make Renee realize there was more to me than my missing lower leg, and the only way I could think to do that was to put her on the spot. "Why did you ask me to join the agency if you have no faith in my ability?"

"You have many outstanding abilities," Renee said so silkily that I could feel my ruffled feathers smoothing. Her gaze didn't waver—almost as if she'd expected this flak from me and had her side of the argument ready to deflect anything I could throw at her.

"We brought you in," she said, "because you know your way around a business statement in several languages. You have access to the defense industry through your father. You have connections with several highly placed branches of society both in New York and in London. And you, more than any of the other girls, can physically alter your looks to fit any situation."

"But…" I said and waited for Renee to fill the space. There was always a damned but.

"Your blinders get in the way. I can't give you a field assignment if I feel I'll be putting you in physical danger."

"We're back to the leg thing again." Didn't everything in my life come back to that blasted leg? If it didn't matter to me, why should it matter to anyone else?

"No, *you're* back to the leg thing again. You made it through training. You've proved you can cope with your handicap." There was actual warmth in Renee's voice as if she really did admire what I'd overcome. She reached for my hand and squeezed it gently. "It's your impetuous tendency that worries me. You grow impatient, you bend the rules and look for the short-cut. There's no place for that in the field. Not when there's so much at stake. Think of it as dressage. Everything has to be precise or you put the whole operation at risk."

"Wait," I said, pulling back, confused by Renee's simultaneous praise and excoriation. "You said you were sending me to work as a groom."

"Then you took offense and didn't let me get to the second part of your mission."

Second part of the mission? Man, I was burning bridges before I even got a foot on them. This was the one thing I kept forgetting about Renee: how good she was at manipulating people to do exactly what she wanted. Now I couldn't refuse the assignment without coming across as a self-pitying spoiled brat.

"I'm sorry." I shrugged. "It's just a groom isn't exactly what I'd had in mind when I'd thought of an undercover assignment."

"In this case, it's the best means for you to gather information on the owners and workers at the Ashcroft Equestrian Center. Grooms are easily overlooked, yet people tend to speak freely around them because the stables are a relaxing environment."

Okay, so this was a test. If I could prove to Renee I could do this, then next time she'd give me something as glamorous as she'd given Porsche Rothschild. I still couldn't believe an airhead like Porsche had gotten to protect the actor Jeremy Reins as her *first* assignment. She'd even gone to the Oscars!

"You've heard of Firewall?"

I nodded, grateful Renee hadn't completely written me off yet. Firewall was a seventeen-hand high fire-red chestnut that loved to jump and made it look easy. Whispers of Olympic gold floated around him. All he needed was a few more years of seasoning and he could be a real contender. "Firewall is a jumper owned by Hardel Industries."

"With his major competitors out of the picture, Firewall comes out as a favorite to take over the summer season."

"Killing to win seems redundant when you have such great horseflesh to do all the work for you."

Renee lifted a shoulder. "Hardel Industries has put a lot of their advertising dollars into promoting Firewall. The more often he makes headlines, the more often the company does. You can't buy that kind of publicity. They can't afford to lose him. Do you know Ross Hardel?"

"I know who he is." I'd met him over ten years ago when his trainer had insisted he improve his seat by taking some dressage lessons. He'd been an arrogant twit then and, if Rubi Cho's gossip column was to be believed, he hadn't changed. Treachery required hard work and Ross Hardel had never liked to work up a sweat. Of course, maybe bumping off the competition was the easiest way for him to win.

"Would he recognize you?" Renee asked.

"I doubt it. We don't run in the same circle." Nor was I the type of woman likely to be photographed clinging to his elbow. He preferred blond Barbie-dolls with IQs smaller than their bustlines. Of course, I'm sure he wasn't seeking intelligent conversation from them.

"Perfect," Renee chirped. "Since both Waldo, Leah Siegel's horse, and Firewall are the top two candidates to become the Horse Ripper's next victim, your job is to make sure nothing happens to them and to report any information you glean about who might have a stake at seeing the competition eliminated."

A secretary who shoveled shit—definitely not what I had in mind when I asked for excitement. Still I put on my best obedient agent face. "That's going to be tough if I'm stuck cleaning stalls while Ross and Leah are hobnobbing poolside."

"Which is why you're to accept any invitation from Ross Hardel."

Oh, God, no. I didn't think I could stand being around that that arrogant prick for five minutes. Being pawed by a pervert was not my idea of fun. Or having him feel my prosthesis and shrink back in disgust. "This guy has a reputation for being a cad."

"And a reputation for a fondness for stable girls. That gives you an in at keeping tabs on him and who might want to do his horse harm."

My fork snapped through the scone and plinked on the gold-trimmed plate. "I certainly hope you're not expecting me to sleep with him!" I didn't need this assignment that badly. "Your whole undercover ploy is going to fall apart if anyone finds out about my leg. There aren't too many one-legged riders around. And he'll have heard of my accident since he was training with my coach at the time." Not to mention that one look at my residual limb usually sent my dates scrambling for excuses to run out the door. Funny how they never called back. Which is why I usually got the leg business out of the way first thing—before I could get attached.

The Mona Lisa half-twist to Renee's mouth had me wondering what she found so amusing. "I don't expect you to prostitute yourself. You can be charming when you put your mind to it, Alexa."

Renee had this groom scenario all figured out. I could accept the assignment and prove myself to her. Or I could pass and very well get skipped over every time. "I'll pack some charm. But wouldn't I be able to get more out of Ross and Leah if I played someone within their circle? I could play the role of an owner. Bring one of my horses along."

"As a groom, you'll have a better chance of extracting information from the help. I'm told they will know all the dirty little secrets the owners try to hide and the goings on behind the scene. The help wouldn't talk to you if you played the role of an owner. From what I understand the horse world is small and almost incestuous."

She got that right. When I'd showed, I'd bumped into the same group of people every weekend. And if someone were to write a book about the lowdown, dirty things that really went on behind the glitz and glamour of the show ring, no one would believe it. Reality was much stranger than fiction.

Renee fingered the edge of the file sitting on the linen tablecloth, and like a good performer, waited until I was practically salivating before opening the red cover. "Ally Cross is to report to Bart Hind at the Ashcroft Equestrian Center just outside of Ashcroft, Connecticut. He's the center's manager and knows nothing about the operation. He's expecting Ally at seven tomorrow morning. Your résumé and job were provided by the center's owner."

"Who is that?"

"Patrick Dunhill."

"The former Olympian?" His black horse Messenger had soared through many of my dreams as I was growing up. He spared no expense on his horses, and his facilities were said to be the Rolls Royce of stables. Maybe this wouldn't be so bad after all.

Renee nodded. "He's made sure you'll be assigned to both Ross Hardel and Leah Siegel's horses. That will allow you to get close to both of them. Alan will provide you with all the necessary paperwork to backstop your Ally Cross identity. No one is to know your true background. Since you used to show, will that be a problem?"

I hadn't stepped foot into a show ring in ten years. Memories were short. "Dressage people and jumping people run in different circles."

"This will require hard physical work, Alexa. Are you up to the job?"

I'd never let my "defective" leg stop me from achieving my goals before. I certainly wouldn't now. If Renee wanted a groom, I could become a groom. "How hard can it be to muck out a stall?"

Chapter 2

My next stop was the elevator hidden behind the rack of shoes and the rows of designer clothes in the closet in Renee's office. I entered my code on the temperature control panel, followed the prompt for a palm print and an iris scan and waited patiently while the computer decided I was indeed who I claimed to be. The panel slid open and I stepped into the car. The glass elevator reminded me of a bullet and was just a little bit disconcerting in the way it blurred the concrete walls as it rushed to the basement level.

Kristi Burke, the undercover stylist, was waiting for me when I got off the elevator. She twisted her hands like a mad scientist facing a brand-new experiment. The lab coat didn't help the effect.

"I had such fun shopping for this assignment," Kristi said, leading me toward the dressing room. Two rolling racks of clothes waited beside a three-way mirror. She sat me in the hairdresser's chair and stood behind me.

"Fun? For *this* assignment?"

Kristi's nose wrinkled cutely as she smiled. "It's not every day I get to dress down someone as gorgeous as you are. I thrive on a challenge." She ran her fingers through strands of my long hair. "First, we need to tone down that beautiful mahogany into something more mousy."

"Mousy?" I didn't like the sound of that.

"I'm going to dye it a flat brown, then overdry it and butcher the ends so they split. Stable girls don't have the money for designer haircuts."

"Sounds absolutely splendid." Oh, yeah, this was definitely a glamorous assignment. "I suppose you want me to bring back my acne and crooked front teeth."

"Could you?" Kristi joked, then knuckled my chin. "Chin up, girl. It's not as bad as it sounds. I'll be able to bring you back to your old self in a couple of hours when your assignment is through."

Chewing on orange-flavored nicotine gum, Kristi chatted about her horrible Internet dating experiences as she dyed and shampooed and snipped and dried my hair into a dull brown frizz that nearly brought tears to my eyes. She took a raggedy scrunchie from one of the drawers by the mirrored table and twisted my hair into a messy bun. "This is the going stableyard style, I'm told. Or try a single braid down your back."

I took in a long drag of air, hating my drab reflection in the mirror. "I think I can manage."

"Good. Now makeup." She showed me how to apply a concoction that dulled my skin and, voila, I was my mother's worst fear come to life. Common. I wanted to treat that poor pasty girl in the mirror to a day at Bliss Spa. She deserved it.

Kristi swiveled the chair around until it was facing the racks of clothes. "Wardrobe's up next. I had a hard time finding jeans that were long enough for you in the leg, but managed to unearth three pairs of Levi's at the Goodwill store."

Goodwill? That was a long way from Barney's on Madison. Oh, this was getting worse by the second. Wearing other people's clothes. I shuddered and scratched at imagined cooties jumping over my skin. Kristi went through the piles of underwear—cotton instead of my usual LaPerla silk—and T-shirts with advertising splashed across the front. She was especially proud of the faded red Barn Goddess one. By the time she closed the zipper on the scuffed L.L. Bean duffel bag, I was near tears. I wasn't vain. Not really. But this was, well, so beneath my station. "If you need anything more, let me know and I'll see what I can dig up."

I hoped to identify the Horse Ripper within a week. I could survive a week in itchy clothes, forking manure. I could. Really. "I think I'm set. Thanks."

Kristi beamed. "My pleasure."

Alan Burke, Kristi's brother, poked his head, dark-brown hair perfectly coiffed, through the dressing room door. "All done?"

"If she was, she'd be with you already, now wouldn't she?" Kristi snapped. Since Kristi had started her smoke-cessation program, she tended to take out her frustrations on her brother. Poor thing.

Ignoring Alan, Kristi reached for a box on top of the dressing table. "I had some darker contacts made with your prescription. Your eyes are such a distinct warm sienna that I figured they might attract attention."

I stashed Kristi's Goodwill-filled duffel bag by the elevator door and made my way to Alan's tech room. The room was filled to the brim with computers, closed-circuit television screens and a wall full of electronic gadgets that would listen, see and record any kind of information you could imagine. I looked at them with envy, knowing a groom wasn't likely to need any of those beauties.

"How's Kyle?" I asked Alan as I took a seat beside him in one of his high-tech chairs. Kyle was a Versace model who lived in Venice. Alan had met him at a recent ball and fallen head over heels in love.

His chocolate-brown eyes drooped at the corners like a disappointed puppy's. "He hasn't called in a while."

"He will. How could he resist a sweetie like you?"

Alan shrugged and got down to the business of going over the technical details of my mission as Ally Cross. "Here's your driver's license, credit card, ATM card, check book, car registration, insurance card. I've also taken the liberty of getting you some of those annoying frequent-shoppers cards. Blockbuster, Stop & Shop, Starbucks. I also found one for an on-line tack shop."

"Impressive." He handed me my new life story stuffed in a faded navy-blue ripcord wallet with Velcro tabs. Swell.

"Everything's backstopped and will stand up to a fairly rigorous investigation." He added a set of keys on a battered brass stirrup keychain to my booty. "Now, I've arranged to have an old Ford Focus modified with a steering wheel accelerator so you can drive it."

Because my right foot was missing, making it difficult to feel the pedal, I had to have a special modification to drive. God, I hated driving, but a groom wasn't likely to arrive at a minimum-wage job in a chauffeur-driven limousine. "You think of everything."

"That's what they pay me for, darling. I also have this." He reached into a drawer and took out a cell phone and a silver locket. He dangled the locket from his index finger. "It doesn't look like much so the risk of having it stolen is practically nil. If you press the front like so." He demonstrated by pressing his thumb against the diamond chip in the middle of the rose scroll and set off an alarm on his computer. "We'll get an SOS signal and be able to come to your rescue. Of course, that'll work better once you're back in the city, but we'll be able to keep track of your movements in Connecticut. It'll just take us longer to get to you."

Somehow that didn't sound as reassuring as it should.

He secured the locket around my neck, then flipped open the phone. "This is really a small computer in disguise. With this, you'll be able to transmit pictures back to me, record conversations should you need to and, using the sliding keypad, record whatever information Renee needs. Plug it in the recharging base every night. At 2:00 a.m., it will automatically transfer whatever you've entered in the computer to our mainframe here. If you need to send something before, just dial Hal's number and he'll take it from there."

Hal being the mainframe. Did I mention Alan loved movies?

"I have a cell phone that can do most of that."

"This one encrypts communications. And this one is registered to Ally Cross."

"Good point."

Alan smiled at me as he handed me the gadget. I stuffed it in the knock-off Dooney & Bourke purse

Kristi had given me as part of my disguise. "You can call me anytime by pressing the number one on the speed dial function." He scooped up a plastic bag at his feet. "Here are a couple of videos from last year's Grand Prix jumping events. That should bring you up-to-date as to who's who in the jumping world. I've also included a book on horse care and grooming. You're a quick study so getting the procedures down pat shouldn't take you long."

I clutched the bag to my chest. Although I'd never personally attempted the feat, cleaning stalls wasn't rocket science. "Great. Thanks."

My last stop was to see Jimmy "The Heartbreaker" Valentine, the agency's personal trainer. I loved him. Of course, so did every other agent, even though "Backbreaker" would be a more apt title for him. He'd worked for the CIA and didn't take any of the crap we dished out. And I can honestly say that none of us have made Jimmy's job easy.

"Hey, sweetheart," Jimmy said as I walked into his gym. He stood in his black shorts and sweat-stained gray T-shirt in front of the mirror doing bicep curls with thirty-pound dumbbells. "How's my girl?"

I fluffed my frizz. "As you can see from Kristi's work of art, I'm going undercover."

He broke out into a face-eating grin. "Congratulations, I know you've been waiting to lead a case for a long time."

"Well, it's not exactly what I had in mind." I

flopped onto a padded bench beside the neat rows of dumbbells on a rack.

"You can do it. I have faith in you."

And his boat-wide smile made shoveling manure suddenly sound like a true opportunity rather than a punishment.

Jimmy was the only one who understood how hard I'd had to work to hide my condition and make my handicap look effortless. He understood because his older brother, Mario, had an arm ripped off above the elbow in a motorcycle accident when he was eighteen. Jimmy had grown up watching Mario endure the long process of fitting an artificial limb and the painful and frustrating hours of practice that went into rehabilitation.

"Hey, guess what?" he said.

"What?"

"Kara's pregnant."

For whatever reason, Jimmy tried to reassure me every time I came to the gym that if an ugly, one-armed, junkyard dog like his brother could find a beautiful woman to marry him, then my finding a partner was definitely in the cards. I'm not sure he understood how superficial men in my social circle could be. "When's the baby due?"

"Right before Christmas."

"Give him my congratulations."

Jimmy put both hands up and backed away. "Heck, no, he's already feeling too proud of himself."

I laughed and picked nervously at a nail that Kristi had so thoughtfully stripped of polish and clipped nearly to the quick. "So, what do you think?"

He frowned and that meant I wouldn't like the answer. "I think you should wear your workout leg."

"Oh, no, please, Jimmy. It's so ugly."

He sat beside me on the bench and wrapped an arm around my shoulders. "The pretty leg will crap out under the load and your residual limb won't be as comfortable. You're heading for hard work, sweetheart. You've gotta take care of yourself."

Coming from Jimmy that didn't feel like a reproach, but the straight truth. I leaned against his shoulder. "How will I hide it? No one's supposed to know who I am."

"Wear pants. Now that it's getting warmer, that's a bummer, but it's the best option. I had Kristi find you a couple of pairs of boots and fitted them with Talux feet."

I sighed. The carbon active heel would help me walk with a fluid, natural motion in a variety of terrains. Most of all, the unit could withstand moderate impact activities that my lifelike, silicone-covered cosmetic leg couldn't—even with its computer controls. But none of that altered the fact that the metal workout leg was butt ugly.

Jimmy scrunched his bushy eyebrows and got all serious on me. "I need you to do me a favor."

"What's that?"

"You gotta promise me you're gonna take care of yourself. Two of my three kids are down with some sort of spring flu, and Linda's driving me crazy as it is. I don't want to have to worry about you, too."

Linda being his wife who only drove him crazy because he loved her so much. Sometimes I wished he wasn't married because, with him, my leg would never be an issue.

"I promise."

"You'll be expending more energy than you're used to, so you're gonna have to increase your calorie intake. If you lose more than five pounds, your prosthesis won't fit properly and you could end up with all sorts of problems."

Keeping weight on wasn't a new issue for me. "I promise I'll eat."

He glared at me with the ball-shrinking gaze that was said to have cowered more than one CIA recruit. He forgot that it didn't work as well on women. "Three squares. No skipping."

I nodded. "I'll pack energy bars."

"That's my girl." He stood up and clamped his hands to his hips. "Now get on the mat and let me take you through the exercises I want you to do every day to keep your core strong and balanced."

He understood me, but that didn't mean he cut me any slack. "Backbreaker," I teased.

His chuckle negated his scowl. "Drop down and give me ten."

* * *

The next morning I glanced at the ugly workout leg leaning against the wall next to my bed at my Darien estate and groaned. *Suck it up, Alexa.* There was no use complaining. The workout leg was the best tool for the job I had to do.

An hour after getting up, I used my Ally Cross frequent-buyer card at a Starbucks before getting onto I-95, treating myself to a grande Americano and choking down an energy bar to keep my promise to Jimmy. In Norwalk, Connecticut, I switched over to the Merritt Parkway because the ride was prettier. My grip on the steering wheel tightened and I belted out a tune at the top of my lungs along with Gwen Stefani on the radio to keep my thoughts from filling my mind with doubts.

In Hartford, I merged onto I-84 and dismissed my building jitters by concentrating on finding the Ashcroft signs. Make that singular. The town was farther and tinier than I'd expected, and the clock on the dashboard was inching closer to seven much too quickly. Showing up late on my first day wasn't the best way to start.

Once I found Ashcroft, I followed the stone wall surrounding the farm for a mile before I turned into the red-bricked pillared entrance to the equestrian center.

To say the place was grand would be an understatement. The state-of-the-art equestrian facility was located on fifty-five rolling acres of woodlands, hills and pastures. Miles of fence made from the white PVC that imitated wood planks and would last forever without needing fresh paint lined the roadway. Definitely not cheap.

The stable was as impressive as the château-inspired mansion where Patrick Dunhill lived. Brick-red paint and white accents kept the color scheme of the main house going. The cupola in the center of the roof matched the mansion's turret. And the covered entry was a nice touch. I left the Focus in the parking lot and, with a bit of trepidation swimming around my stomach—which I blamed on the large cup of coffee rather than nerves—I headed for the barn office.

I could do this. I could.

Bart Hind, the manager, sat behind a black metal desk, barking into the phone to what, I gathered, was the feed supplier. His skin looked slept in, the folds and wrinkles ironed in as if he'd stayed too long in one spot. His hair had once been brown, but now was so shot with white that it looked dusty. He wore navy work pants and a plaid work shirt with the sleeves rolled up to his elbows.

"Who are you?" he growled as he slammed down the phone.

"Ally Cross. You were expecting me this morning."

He glanced at the large clock on the wall and grunted. I'd thankfully found the place and squeaked in a few minutes early. He sidestepped from behind the desk. With a hand gesture, he told me to follow him. His work boots thunked on the concrete floor as he made his way into the barn.

I'd always loved the smell of stables—hay, sweet feed and leather. But there was no time to admire the bouquet. I had to pay attention to Hind's rapid-fire instructions.

"You'll have six horses." He chewed every word as if it were the toughest cut of meat, then spit it out like gristle. "You're expected to muck out their stalls, feed, groom, rotate them into paddocks and get them ready for their owners according to schedule. You work five till whenever the job's done. Horses don't care about a clock. Mondays are off."

"Where will I find this schedule?" I asked, head spinning just a little bit.

"In the tack room and feed room."

He stuck two fingers in his mouth and whistled. A head popped up from a stall up the aisle and he gestured the woman over. "This is the new girl. Show her around. She's got the Siegel and all five Hardel horses."

The girl's gray eyes widened behind her water-spotted glasses. "Sure. No problem."

And just like that Bart Hind was gone, leaving me standing there as if I were a cartoon character suspended above a canyon with nowhere to go but down.

"I'm Dawn Waller," the girl said, offering her

hand. Her head full of droopy caramel curls bounced with each of her steps. Kristi had hit the wardrobe right on the nose, judging by Dawn's outfit—jeans, boots, faded navy T-shirt.

"Ally Cross." The calluses at the base of each of Dawn's fingers scratched at my too-soft palm. I let go of her hand as politely as I could.

"Don't take it personally," Dawn said, leading me down the wide roughened-concrete center aisle. "Bart's a regular jackass. But he's not here for his personality. Mr. Dunhill cares about the horses. Period. He couldn't care less about the people. Unless they're helping pay the bills, of course."

She waved her arm at the stalls, whose varnished pine gleamed gold under the daylight overheads running the length of the barn. "We have thirty-six stalls. Two are empty at the moment. But they won't stay that way for long. Mr. Dunhill has a waiting list a mile long. Other than Hind, there are six grooms— well, six now that you're here—a maintenance assistant and two trainers. You'll meet them later."

Dawn introduced me to a couple of grooms, then moved on to the tack room. The pine-sided room had a utility counter and sink. A large white board listed each horse down the left-hand side and the horse's training and turnout schedule on the right. A multipronged hook hung from the ceiling to clean bridles. Each station had a saddle rack, saddle pad rack and a bridle rack and a built-in tack trunk. Separating each station was a locker with each owner's name printed by a label maker. I'd have to find time to inspect their contents and see if they turned up anything related to the Horse Ripper.

Dawn showed me a similar white board in the feed room delineating each horse's rations. She pointed out the two wash stalls with hot water and heat lamps and the six grooming cross-tie areas with nonskid pads.

"These horses are quite pampered," I said.

"You ain't seen nothing yet! Some owners bring in an equine psychologist and a massage therapist. There's even one who calls in a certified hypnotist to make sure her darling's happy. Can you believe it?"

Well, yeah, I could. I got massage therapy for my horse Persephone every week now that she was growing old. "Amazing."

"Some people definitely have too much money to burn." As we reached another section of stalls, Dawn cupped a hand over her mouth and whispered, "Watch out for Erin."

"Why?"

"The bitch is a professional suck-up. She thinks ratting on us is part of her job."

Dawn gave the stall wall a quick jab. Erin popped up.

"Erin Mays," Dawn said. "Meet the new girl. Ally Cross."

Erin's wide-set green eyes squinted at me through

the open stall door with the feral intensity of a killer iguana. Her brown French braid started right at her forehead, giving it the look of a ruff on top of her head. I almost expected it to pop up and spread like it did on nature shows.

"Nice to meet you," I said and smiled as cheerfully as I could.

"Same here," she said with all the warmth of wet wood.

As we moved on, I couldn't help rolling my shoulders to dislodge the spear of ill will shot in my direction.

Dawn was back to her conspiratorial voice. "Katelyn Tierney's voice is all honey, but don't let that fool you. She's not going to be happy to see you."

"Why not?"

"She's been maneuvering to get herself assigned to Ross Hardel's horses, and here you are a newbie taking over her coveted spot. They're hers this morning, and she's not going to give them up without a fight." Dawn smirked. "She has a crush on him."

"Who? Ross Hardel?"

Dawn nodded. "She's sadly mistaken if she thinks a romp between the sheets is going to get her a ring on the finger."

"Great." Would Katelyn's infatuation make getting close to Ross difficult? With two out of five grooms wanting to cut me to pieces before they'd even met me, gathering the underground gossip Renee wanted wasn't going to be quite as easy as I'd imagined. But Dawn seemed open enough. I'd have to cultivate her friendship and see what I could unearth about the goings-on at the Ashcroft Equestrian Center.

"Katelyn?" Dawn said to the blonde spreading wood shavings on a freshly cleaned stall floor. "Here's Ally. The new girl. I'll let you show her what Waldo and the Hardel horses need."

I had a bad feeling about Katelyn. Her smile reminded me of a shark—the type that knew the difference between a seal and a swimmer and went after the swimmer every time.

She handed me a pitchfork and said, "Sink or swim, honey. I haven't got the time or the inclination to hold your hand."

Welcome to the team, Ally.

Chapter 3

Standing on the concrete aisle, I held on to the pitch-fork with perhaps a tad too much force as Katelyn left me in her dust. Sink or swim, Katelyn had said. I could already taste the water filling my lungs and the need to put out an SOS screamed inside me like a little girl drowning. I fingered the locket at my throat. *Take it easy.* No need to call in the cavalry yet. This was no different from societal posturing. And I'd managed that dance often enough. I'd probably act territorial, too, if I felt someone was poaching on my domain.

Okay, since Katelyn was going to let me flounder on my own, the first thing I had to do was figure out what I was expected to accomplish. Hind's list of tasks was long, but rather slim on details. I headed to the tack room and checked the board. I discovered that my charges had all had their morning rations and their morning grooming. I was expected to have the stalls cleaned before the lunch feed and Cielo Azur ready for the trainer by one.

Feeling a bit more oriented, I trekked back to my section of stalls and dug in.

Within fifteen minutes my back and legs were crying uncle from all the unfamiliar bending and scooping, and I had a line of fresh blisters at the base of my fingers that made each heft of the pitchfork pure agony. Even Jimmy's torturing workouts had never made me as aware of my hamstrings as I was now. If I moved too fast, I just knew my back was going to spasm.

By stall number four, I was ready to close my eyes and let the jets in my hot tub knead away the tight knots in every one of my muscles. That little fantasy popped at the sound of Bart Hind's voice barking at me.

"What the hell are you doing?"

I looked down at the sinus-clearing, urine-soaked pile of shavings precariously balanced on the pitchfork and had to bite back the automatic remark of, 'What does it look like I'm doing?' and said, "Mucking out Bay Bridge Bandit's stall."

"Your résumé says you have five years' professional experience. At doing what?"

Managing a multimillion-dollar foundation, jack. That's more money and responsibility than you'll ever see. But of course, that wasn't the right answer. "Taking care of horses."

"Where? In Fantasy Land? Because in the real world, there's a timetable. And you're behind schedule. A five-year-old could work faster than you are."

"Sorry, I'll kick it up another notch." I shoved the pitchfork into a pile of wet shavings with renewed enthusiasm. Still, I couldn't help the first-day-at-school feeling, when you don't know anyone but want everyone to like you, especially the teacher.

"Sorry isn't going to get you anywhere," Hind said, looking a bit Napoleonic with his swept-back forelock and a hand planted across his slight paunch as if it ached. "I don't care who you slept with to get this job. If you don't work to my standards, you'll be out on your ass before you have a chance to go cry in your sugar daddy's lap."

He thought I'd slept with Patrick Dunhill to get this lowly job? Ew, gross. The guy had to be over fifty and showed every year of it. As much as I'd like a hot and heavy affair, I'd rather do it with someone closer to my age and easier on the eyes.

Hind pointed at the black horse across the aisle. "Magnus was supposed to get his midmorning hay half an hour ago, and you were supposed to be done with stalls before then. And if that's what you call grooming, I really don't know what you did to get your recommendations."

As if Magnus agreed, he pawed at his bedding. I ground my back teeth and hung on to my cool. "It's taking me a little time to get oriented to where everything is."

Hind made a noise that was half growl, half chuff. "I'll cut you some slack for today." He jerked his chin in the direction of the bedding in Bandit's stall. "Don't be stingy on the shavings. Mr. Dunhill wants the horses comfortable. Get Magnus's hay. Now. And groom him properly."

"Yes, sir." Honest, I tried to keep the biting edge out of my voice.

His scowl deepened, giving him a Cro-Magnon ridge that told me I wasn't making a friend. "Make sure everyone's in on time. Azur's hard to catch. Take a handful of grain."

"I'm on it." This time I *was* thankful for the tip.

After stuffing Magnus's hay net with hay, I grabbed a lead line and the leather halter marked with Cielo Azur's name and made my way to the network of paddocks. Might as well get the tough one out of the way first.

I rested my foot on the bottom rung of the fence to take the pressure off my throbbing residual limb and took a minute to bask in the breeze that dried the sweat sticking my shirt to my skin. I closed my eyes, fantasizing about lavender French-milled soap, moisturizing shampoo and the shell-pink silk teddy and tap pants I'd bought in Paris and hadn't yet gotten to wear. Not that there was anyone special to wear them for right now. With a sigh, I stared at the dozen or so horses grazing in the various enclosures with no idea as to which one I was supposed to put in which stall.

Dawn popped up beside me, startling me. "What's up?"

"You were right about Katelyn."

Dawn snorted as gustfully as a horse in a dusty arena. "She's been bitching about you all morning. She thinks you're competition."

"For what?"

"Ross Hardel."

"Yeah, right," I scoffed.

"You'd be surprised."

Here was a chance to tap into some gossip. "He has a thing for the help?"

"Not all grooms. His grooms. He wants to be sure his horses get the best of care."

"Broken hearts get him that? I'd think that'd make him worry about revenge."

Dawn snorted. "But a girl in love'll go out of her way to please him."

"Ah." I breathed in the scent of spring grass. "It's so pretty here."

"Yeah, just wait till the owners show up. It won't seem quite as serene then."

"How so?"

"All those Park Avenue princesses can be bitches. Not that the guys are much better. Divas all of them." Dawn bobbled her head from side to side, taking on a whiny voice. "Do this. Do that. Take care of me first. No, me, I'm more important. Bunch of spoiled brats."

Was that how I came across to my stable hand? I rolled my aching shoulders, hoping Dawn would take my self-conscious blush for sunburn. "With the competition moving north for the summer, is anyone worried about the Horse Ripper showing up here? I mean what with Firewall and Waldo both training here."

"Naw, Mr. Dunhill hired a security guard to patrol at night. And there's security cameras everywhere. I don't think he'll show up here."

"There were guards at the showgrounds in Florida," I pointed out.

"Showgrounds are more confusing. Strangers come and go. Here everyone knows everyone. It'd be hard to get to a horse without being noticed."

Unless you were an insider. "Makes you wonder who could do such a thing, doesn't it?"

Dawn pushed her glasses back up her nose. "Doesn't surprise me at all. I've seen owners stick electrodes up their horses' butts or noses to electrocute them for insurance money. There was this vet who stole horses, spray painted their markings with Rust-Oleum and sold them to unsuspecting clients in a different city."

"He got away with it?"

Dawn shook her head. "Not for long. He's in jail now."

"And drugging's nothing new," I added.

"Nope. Happens all the time."

"Do you think anyone here's hard up enough to want to get Waldo or Firewall out of the way?"

Dawn shrugged. "There's certainly enough jealousy flying around, so you never know."

"Yeah?"

Dawn laughed. "You have no idea. It's like a soap opera with all the bed-hopping and horse-trading."

"Dish," I said, hoping to narrow down my list of suspects.

She shook the halter in her hand and popped over the fence. "Gotta get my horses in before B. Hind barks at me."

"Yeah, me too. Which one's Cielo Azur?"

Dawn pointed at a small gray horse—in the farthest paddock, of course. "The dappled filly. She's a bit hard to catch."

I scooped out the handful of feed in my pocket. "I brought a bribe."

"Good move."

"What about the Hardel horses?" I asked. I'd seen Firewall in photos all decked out in show attire, but at pasture, he was just another red horse.

Dawn pointed out each one, as well as Waldo. "Waldo's pretty well behaved. Firewall wants to lead and will drag you if you give him half a chance. Trademark Infringement bites and Bay Bridge Bandit kicks."

"Hey, thanks."

"No problem. Katelyn needs an attitude adjustment. She's not a team player, if you know what I mean."

I didn't, but nodded anyway to show that I was and prove I belonged in this dead-end job. Dawn tossed a salute my way and trotted toward a group of horses. "Catch ya later."

This horse business had me way over my head. Renee must be laughing in her tea, I thought, shaking my head as I made my way to Azur.

At the sight of someone entering her paddock, the mare popped her head up. Staring right at me, she wrung her tail, did a splendid turn on the haunches and took off.

Just as I reached her, she galloped off again. I almost had her cornered when I slipped and fell on my butt—on a fresh pile of horse apples, of course. I swear the little hussy smiled as she trotted away. This gray matador was enjoying the game a little too much and I was ready to choke her with the lead line, never mind the fact I couldn't get close enough to her to accomplish the feat.

I sat there, too tired to move. Azur studied me and looked disappointed that I wasn't playing anymore. She bent down, chewed off a bit of grass, then made her way closer to me, bite by bite.

"I know your type," I said, thinking of high school and the games girls played there. "You like to bully. But you're picking on the wrong person. Renee expects me to fail, but I'm actually really good at playing games. And I've been doing it a lot longer than you have."

Azur's ears flicked back and forth. Watching her nimble lips parcel out a juicy section of grass and hack it off with her big teeth, I chewed the inside of my cheek. This four-legged, four-year-old with a smaller brain than mine controlled the situation. How was that for irony?

Horses, being herd animals, have a strong sense of pecking order. Which, come to think of it, wasn't so different from high school cliques. All I had to do was let her know who was the boss.

The horse-care book Alan had given me explained about the zones of influence. At first I wondered if I'd gotten my boss-horse signals crossed because Azur didn't respond, except to walk away, swishing her tail. Then a burst of pleasure exploded inside me as she stopped, then lowered her head, chewing in a sign of submission. By the time I slipped the halter over her receptive head, we both knew I was lead mare and I felt much better about my chances of success as a groom.

The feeling of elation lasted only until I reached the stable. I clipped Azur to the cross ties in a grooming stall and was attempting to lift one of her feet so I could pick it out when a voice came up behind me.

"I've been watching you."

Peering over my shoulder, I looked into a pair of deep brown eyes that were slicing and dicing me as finely as any Cuisinart blade. This couldn't be good.

"Excuse me?" I straightened and dumped the hoof pick in the brush caddy.

He wore old leather boots on his wide feet, brown breeches that had seen better days and a beige polo shirt smeared with horse slobber on the shoulder. Physically, he didn't look much older than thirty. But something in his eyes seemed to carry the scars of a hard life and shouted, "You can't touch me."

Grant Montney, the trainer. I recognized him from the background file Alan had given me. He had a reputation for being champion of the underdog. He lived in a trailer behind the barn and worked at this center because Patrick Dunhill indulged him in his obsession to fix the broken horses he rescued with free room and board for both horses and man.

"Who are you?" His voice was as sharp as his confrontational attitude.

"Ally Cross. I'm the new groom." To prove my point, I picked up a rubber currycomb and attacked the mud caked on Azur's coat.

"Where did you work before?"

I shot him a look packed with attitude. "Why the third-degree?"

Azur turned her head as if she found the conversation fascinating.

"I like to know who works with my horses."

"I worked at Applewood Farm for Belinda Carmichael." Belinda was another of Renee's agents. I suspected she would have this assignment if she weren't seven months pregnant. If Hind, or anyone else, called to check up on my references, Belinda would back up what was on the résumé.

"I know Belinda," he said with a nod. "Nice girl. What'd you do for her?"

"Took care of her show horses."

"Why'd you leave?"

"Belinda's pregnant and decided not to show this year."

He eyed me as if I was horseflesh at auction and he'd found a major conformation fault. I prided myself on holding my squirming to a minimum and continued to lift clouds of dust from Azur's coat.

"So you've prepped horses for the show ring." Not a question, I noticed, but a fact that if I agreed to I'd probably have to prove.

"Yes." Gulp.

"Braid Azur's mane for her lesson."

Crap. "Braid?"

He jerked his chin at Azur's neck. "Give me a dressage braid."

Dressage braid. Double gulp. I hadn't gotten to that part of the manual yet. I'd always paid someone to do the tedious work of braiding for me and I had no idea how to do those button beauties. But I wasn't a quitter. The last time I'd shown Persephone, she'd worn a running braid. I'd done something similar to my hair often enough to bluff my way through it. No braid was going to lose me this assignment.

I dropped the brush into the caddy, reached for a mane comb and attacked Azur's silver mane. His stare was so rimy that my fingers felt as if they were encased in ice.

"You had a good showing in Florida," I said, hoping conversation would throw off the pinch of his concentrated stare.

"I had good horseflesh to work with."

"You were lucky to escape the Horse Ripper."

"Luck had nothing to do with it."

This guy was tougher to crack than a Brazil nut. "There's a rumor he's after any horse that wins a jumping Grand Prix. Since you're coaching the two horses most likely to win at the horse show next week, aren't you worried?"

"You should be the one to worry."

"Me?"

"Grooms here are expected to show discretion. Hind hears you gossiping and you'll find yourself out the door."

Great. The last thing I needed was for him to report me to Hind. I opted for silence. When I finished the braid, there wasn't an elastic handy, so I pinched the ends between my fingers and glanced at my tormentor over my shoulder. "Anything else?"

"I've seen better." He shook his head. "I can't

imagine why Dunhill would entrust the care of expensive horses to an inept novice."

I frowned and wanted desperately to shake off the flash of myself at fourteen, ugly and awkward, always having to do better to meet my parents' impossible standards and never quite being able to. "I don't know who you are to be passing judgment on me like this."

"What's the real reason you're here?" he asked again, ignoring my concern.

One thing I'd learned growing up was to read people and give them what they expected. Want to get noticed? Show off some flesh and throw your shoulders back as if you owned the world. Want no one to realize you're around? Wear baggy clothes, flat shoes and hang your head. What Grant Montney wanted was an excuse to either champion me or kick me around. I took a calculated risk.

"You want the truth?" I asked, running a tentative hand down Azur's neck. I hung my head practically to her mane.

Montney tilted his head to one side and crossed his arms beneath his chest. "That would be refreshing."

"The truth is that I'm a screwup." I kept my voice low and my eyes darted up and down the aisle as if I didn't want anyone else hearing about my shortcomings. "My parents kicked me out of the house because I failed out of school. I had nowhere to go, so Belinda took me in. Now with the baby coming." I shrugged the way people did when they wanted others to believe that whatever they were dismissing was no big deal but really was. I should have gotten to go to the Oscars instead of Porsche.

"I had to move on. She knows Patrick Dunhill and put in a word for me. She gave me this chance and I'm trying really hard not to blow it." I slanted him my most innocent look. "Have I done anything wrong with Azur or with any of the horses?"

He didn't say anything for a long while and I was starting to think my little act had failed to make an impression.

"The jury's still out." He approached Azur's side and ran a hand down her front leg, stopping at her fetlock. "Squeeze here and she'll pick up her foot."

And like magic, she did.

"Thanks," I said, containing my elation at this small triumph over the trainer. "I love working with horses. I really am trying to do a good job."

He nodded before heading back to wherever he'd come from. "See that you do."

A short while later, a shrill whistle pierced my musings of bubble baths and silk sheets as I clipped a lead line to Harrison's halter for his daily constitutional as outlined on the chore chart. I looked around half-expecting my stablehand's Jack Russell terrier to come romping up the aisle. Then I remembered I wasn't at my estate and I was the groom.

"Hey, you!" A thunderous voice rolled from behind me at the back doors of the stable. I fervently hoped I wasn't the one in trouble—again. Bart Hind had already found a dozen ways to criticize me. If I wasn't more careful, I'd end up heading home before I even got to unpack my suitcase.

The black silhouette at the door strode into the light, and I froze when I realized Ross Hardel was stomping his way toward me.

The last time I'd seen him was at a riding lesson at my dressage coach's stable more than ten years ago—preaccident. He'd been an obnoxious teenage twit two inches shorter than me, all skinny arms and knobby knees. Now look at him. Six feet of hard, lean muscle and brooding bad boy.

And if you believed the gossip rags—every woman's dream. Yeah, right. None of my dreams involved a one-night stand, but then, I had high standards. I still wanted to believe I had a chance at a relationship that lasted longer than a bump in the night with a stranger.

His Vogel boots, polished to a mirror finish and undoubtedly custom-made, struck the concrete with understated power. He reeked of cool aloofness, yet more electricity flashed from the killer blue of his eyes than a nuclear power plant.

And all that potent energy was directed at me.

Even though he looked as irritable as Nat in full PMS mode, even with everything I knew about him, something in me just kind of gave as he got nearer.

Curiosity, undoubtedly. My downfall, I'll admit. He was probably used to that reaction from women, likely even expected it, and for some reason that irked me. Having my hormones scramble to attention for a guy who was whistling at me as if I were a dog doubled the insult.

"Surely you can't be whistling at me," I said, tapping my chest with the tips of my fingers as he stopped in front of me and hitched his fists on his hips like some sort of bloodthirsty pirate.

"What the hell are you doing?"

His voice rumbled like thunder and rolled inside me in a way I found disconcerting. Did everyone pick on the new girl or was it just me?

"What does it look like I'm doing?" I shot before I could stop myself. In my defense, I'd already had a backbreaker of a day and it wasn't over yet.

His eyes narrowed. "Where's Mandy?"

"Who's Mandy?"

"The girl who takes care of my horses."

"That would be me."

"You're not Mandy."

"I believe we've already established that."

His scowl deepened. "What happened to Mandy?"

"She left?" I raised both eyebrows and widened my eyes in a duh motion.

"Why?" He asked the question as if somehow Mandy's departure was part of a conspiracy against him.

I dismissed the follow with a half snort. "Do I look like directory assistance?"

"Whatever happened to yes, sir?"

I scratched Magnus's velvety muzzle. "I believe Lincoln freed the slaves a while back."

He shook his head. "Where did they find you?"

"Me?" I shot him my best country bumpkin smile. "Why, I'm fresh off the hay truck."

He scowled again, definitely not amused.

"I don't want anyone but Mandy taking care of Magnus." He spoke to me, but his gaze flicked over Magnus as if my mere presence at his side had somehow damaged the horse.

"You're out of luck, then," I said, urging Magnus forward, "because she's gone and I'm it."

"Magnus is special." Ross's hand reached for the lead line, forcing us both to halt and me to let go of my hold.

"So are all my charges." I stuck my hands in my jeans pockets, puffing out my chest and raising my chin.

Magnus nickered softly and, with nimble lips, sucked up the sugar cube in Ross's palm.

"You're going to rot his teeth," I said, taking in Ross's mink-brown hair, the stretch of custom-tailored breeches over ripped thighs and the breadth of shoulders beneath the navy polo shirt. A body like that was wasted on someone like him.

"He's recovering," Ross said with warmth I hadn't

expected. His big hand cupped Magnus's jaw and Magnus leaned his head into the caress. "He needs extra pampering."

"Recovering from what?"

"An accident."

My ears perked up. Renee hadn't mentioned a Magnus in her rundown of the Horse Ripper's victims, but then he was still alive and the others were dead. "What happened to him?"

"You're full of questions." His gaze lasered into me, leaving traces of heat where it landed.

Curiosity, as I said, was my downfall, and what Renee counted on to get a lead on the Horse Ripper. I shrugged as if I didn't care. "If I'm caring for him, I should know all there is to know about him."

"He needs a consistent routine and extra care. Mandy knew what to do."

Not rolling my eyes took everything I had. "It's not rocket science. If you tell me what he needs, I can take care of your horse the way you want."

His gaze speared me again. The newspaper photographs had definitely missed something. The blue flame of his irises went right through me, causing a slow burn I'd all but given up on ever feeling. Too bad the flamethrower was a shallow playboy. He'd take one look at my prosthesis and move on to leggier pastures. But I didn't need to get in his pants, just earn his confidence. "I don't like the way you're looking at me."

The slow glide of his gaze studied me from frizzy head to scuffed boot toe. "I'm not sure I like what I'm seeing."

Of course not. I wasn't blond or buxom and had a higher IQ than he was used to. The hairs on the back of my neck rose and a growl started to form in my chest. "I've been around horses a long time."

"I'm sure you have. It's not that I don't trust you, but" He shrugged. "I don't know you."

"On the other hand, your reputation precedes you." I don't know how Renee expected me to charm Ross Hardel when all my best features were hidden beneath Goodwill clothes, a bad dye job and eau de manure.

He shot me a wry smile. "Then you know I expect the best for my horses."

And a few personal extras from the groom.

He hadn't exactly hit on me, though, had he? For some reason I found that mildly irritating.

I still had two horses to groom and tack before five. "Magnus is due for his walk. Since I'm below par, he's all yours." Saving half an hour of hand walking was just fine with me.

Before Ross could answer, another whistle ripped through the electric eddy already swirling around the stable. Bart Hind this time, standing outside his office door in his usual Napoleonic stance. Was that Katelyn slinking out of his office? I'd bet a week's pay she'd just finished complaining about my work, hoping she'd take over the horses she coveted.

"Sounds like he went to the same charm school you did," I mumbled, giving Magnus's neck a parting pat before starting in Bart's direction.

"Don't you walk away from me," Ross said. "We're not done here."

I pretended to give his insipid command thought. "Let's see. Um. Paycheck or attitude?" I shrugged and pointed a thumb over my shoulder at Hind. "Paycheck wins."

Ross's skewering stare as I walked away from him made me feel naked. I tried to ignore the burn of his gaze, but it seared me until I reached Hind's office.

"What's all the shouting about?" Hind asked.

Shouting? "Mr. Hardel is upset because I'm not Mandy." Poor Ross would have to get laid elsewhere tonight.

Hind frowned. "Any questions are to be directed to me."

"Yes, sir."

"You'd do well to remember that the owner's always right."

Against my will, my eyebrows lifted. "Even when he's wrong?"

"Especially when he's wrong."

That was one hell of a philosophy. Keeping an impassive face and my mouth from dropping all the way down to the spotless concrete floor took all the muscle control I had left. "About Mandy—" I misdirected his glance to the aisle with a sweep of one hand, and with the other scooped up the master key I'd seen him use on an owner's locker earlier and pocketed it. Easier to search the lockers with a key than attempting to finesse the locks open with a pick.

"I'll take care of the situation. Leah Siegel is running half an hour late. Make sure Waldo's warmed up for her five-o'clock lesson."

Dismissed again. I wasn't sure I could get used to this cockroach treatment.

As I slid past Ross and Hind discussing Mandy's departure, Ross's gaze flashed with potent anger that said he wasn't through with me. Not by a long shot.

Chapter 4

By seven that evening, I was one giant bruise. Muscles I never knew existed wailed every time I moved. My hair, my skin, my clothes were filthier than I'd ever imagined they could get. I wasn't cut out for this type of work. I needed food, aspirin, a massage—and a shower—in no specific order.

As I put away the last of my tools, Dawn poked her head into the tack room. "Ready to call it a day?"

I was ready five hours ago. "All set."

"Give me a lift and I'll show you to the house."

Until this moment I hadn't given housing more than a passing thought, and even then I'd imagined myself at a hotel soaking my weary bones in a hot tub.

Dawn flopped down on the passenger's seat and grinned at me as if swallowing a private joke. "So you survived your first day."

"Looks like it."

"You didn't do so bad." Dawn pointed out the windshield. "Drive around the back of the barn. We're not supposed to park in the owners' lot."

I cranked over the engine and put the car in drive, faking foot motion so Dawn wouldn't notice the hand accelerator cleverly hidden in the padded steering-wheel cover.

"I've seen girls quit in tears before Hind even finished his introductory bark," Dawn said with a bit too much gleam in her eyes.

"Is that why everyone's been avoiding me?"

Dawn brayed. "We've learned to give it a day or two before warming up. Like I said, Hind isn't easy to take."

I'd have to ask Alan to check into the turnover. Maybe that was how the Horse Ripper was slipping in to supposedly secure stables. "Why is Hind so hard?"

"Well," Dawn lowered her voice as if someone else could overhear. "The story is that years ago he was on course to be a great eventer. But he was stupid. Let his dick take over his brain and slept with his sponsor's trophy wife. The old geezer caught them rolling in the hay and shot Hind. From what I heard, his knee was shattered. The knee healed, but Hind was never the same."

I supposed he could have been handsome when he was younger. I couldn't see it now. "Wow, that is so the last position I'd picture Hind in."

Dawn smirked. "I don't want to imagine that, either! Story goes he took to drinking after that to dull the pain."

"How'd he end up here, then?"

"He's a friend of Grant Montney, the trainer. He got him the job here."

"Is he still drinking?" If he was, it made blackmail a possibility. On the other hand, the second chance could be the reason he was so fiercely protective of his territory.

"If he is, he's discreet about it."

The house was hidden at the edge of the woods near the back of the property. From the outside, it looked as if it had sat there forever. The roof and porch sagged like a hammock. The white paint looked gray and the red trim dull and in need of touch-ups. A collection of five cars in worse shape than the rust bucket I was driving lined the driveway.

"Park anywhere," Dawn said. "We're not fussy."

Given the condition of the house, that was probably a survival technique. Don't expect anything and you won't be disappointed. I stopped behind a white pickup with more scratches than paint.

Dawn threw open the creaky front door and said, "Home, sweet home! I'll show you to your room."

The scent of sautéing onions filled the air and

set my stomach growling. I hadn't eaten anything all day except two energy bars. Jimmy would not be happy.

Dawn led me up the narrow stairway. Pipes moaned and groaned inside the wall. Halfway down the hall she said, "Here you go. Sorry about the mess. I guess Mandy didn't bother cleaning before she left."

I took a peek inside and wanted to cry. "How fast did she leave?"

"Too fast."

"What happened?"

Shrugging, she tossed her hands up. "With Hind, who knows?"

Plain white walls framed an unmade bed. Its yellowing sheets and utilitarian brown blanket were thrown about as if someone had left in hurry—or in anger. Was Mandy forced to leave against her wishes because of my assignment? I hoped not.

The closet hung open and a free-fall sculpture of metal hangers cascaded from the wooden rod. Candy wrappers, used tissues and wadded-up papers overflowed from the garbage can by the distressed dresser whose drawers were in various stages of closure. Something small and black skittered across the wide pine board floor and under the bed. I squealed.

Dawn laughed in great goose honks as if sharing a room with insects was normal. "Bathroom's down the hall. Sounds like Katelyn's hogging it as usual. It's Tomas's turn to cook, so you don't want to be late."

"I take it he's a good cook." I searched for a clean spot to put my bag and settled on the dresser top.

"If you like spicy food. We take turns making dinner. You'll fill Mandy's spot. You can cook, can't you?"

"If it comes in a box, I can figure it out." I did cook for myself once in a while, but somehow I doubted that anyone here would appreciate the finer points of lobster-mushroom crêpes or ahi tuna with spinach en papillote.

Dawn's mouth twisted in disappointment. "Breakfast and lunch are on your own. Clean the bathroom and kitchen as you go. Someone comes in to take a layer of dust once every couple of weeks. Laundry's in the basement. You'll need your own soap and such."

With that, she closed the door and left me in the middle of my new hovel. I looked around at the filth and cursed Renee for dropping me into this nightmare.

As much as I wanted to collapse on the springless mattress, there was no way I could sleep on these dirty sheets.

With a sigh I forced myself to strip the bed, wishing I could just send them out to the cleaners and have them returned with a lavender rinse.

I groaned as I gathered the sheets. Definitely not silk. Some sort of polyester blend with a two-digit thread count from the feel of it. It's only for a few days, I reminded myself. I could stand anything for a few days. That's how I got through therapy—one day at a time. As I straightened, I winced at the muscles spasming in my lower back.

I had more money than I could spend in a lifetime, I thought, making my way to the first floor. I didn't need this or Renee's approval. I could achieve some good without being part of her secret club.

Except that my stubborn pride wouldn't let me quit.

I found the door to the basement. My nose wrinkled as the stale, humid air of the cellar hit me. This couldn't be healthy. I'd need a full spa treatment when I got back home. Maybe even fumigation.

So I'd had a less-than-stellar first day on the job. That was normal. Expected even. No one could know all the ins and outs and quirks on the first day. Tomorrow I'd do better.

The thought cheered me until I reached the third step from the bottom and something hard crashed against my ankle, knocking me off balance.

I tumbled down the last two wooden stairs, ending up in a heap of stinky sheets. Whatever had hit me collided with something else in a crash of plastic and cardboard against concrete. When I looked up, two glowing green eyes stared at me out of a fluff of ghost-gray fur under the utility sink and growled like some sort of possessed demon. A yellow box of detergent lay on its side, as did a blue bottle of fabric softener. A line of spilled white powder detergent separated me from the cat.

"I feel your pain," I said to the cat and pushed myself to my hands and knees. "Disturbing your little corner of hell is the last thing on my mind."

Demon-beast spat at me and added a double swipe of paws to make sure he left an impression.

The lights went out and the squeak of stairs registered at the same time as the "oh crap" of realization hit me. I should have remembered Jimmy's lessons: Always be aware of your surroundings and always be prepared to protect your vulnerable parts. A foot connected painfully with my butt, sending me sprawling through the dark right into the path of ripping claws. The stinging triple strike of sharpened hooks would look like red war paint for days and riled up my survival instincts.

Another of Jimmy's lessons: the most important weapon in a brawl is the will to win.

A flush of adrenaline suppressed the smarting pain of my bleeding cheek. I smelled sweat and something flowery. I rolled onto my back and kicked out blindly at what sounded like loose change in a pocket. My boots connected with legs, knocking my opponent off her feet. As she went down, she swore. So far no weapon, but that didn't mean she wasn't packing. I'd noticed that all the grooms carried utility knives.

I scrambled to my feet and reached for the light switch. Evasion was usually the best option, but I needed to know who was jumping me and why. A fist jarred into my spine, stealing my breath and throwing me forward. I splayed my hands to stop myself from falling, but still kissed the spider-web-coated wall of the basement, tasting blood when my molars sank into my tongue. Spitting out dusty silk, I whirled to face my opponent, bringing up a knee and getting an umph of expelled air as a reward for connecting with soft stomach.

Tuning into the sound of jingling coins, I threw a right palm strike at my attacker's face and kicked her feet out from under her. She went down like a sack of grain. I finished with a stomp to her rib cage.

Groaning, she flung her arms back and attempted to swim away.

"Not so fast." I reached down and grabbed the front of her T-shirt, then lifted her off the floor. Her arms flayed and a rain of powder hit my face, burrowed into the cat scratches and stung like hell. The second volley found my eyes and had me swearing.

I tried to hang on to her T-shirt, but she planted both sneakered feet into my stomach and flung me like a pumpkin in a catapult. I crashed against the dryer, sending demon-beast on another flurry of spits and paw bats.

Ignoring pain and exhaustion, I picked myself up the floor and tore up the stairs after my attacker. I crashed into her just as she opened the door and pinned her half in, half out.

"What the hell was that all about?" Breathing hard, I got in Erin's face.

She shoved at me, jade-cold anger hardening her eyes. "It's your fault. I heard Hind."

"My fault for what?"

"That Mandy left."

"I don't even know who Mandy is." But I would definitely ask Alan to find out. She was causing a lot of problems for someone who wasn't even here.

"I *heard* Hind with Mr. Dunhill. Hind said he didn't like being told who to hire."

That would definitely give Hind a reason to ride me as hard as he was. "That doesn't mean I got Mandy fired."

"She didn't do what they said she did."

"Which was?"

"Putting Cocoa Crème into Messenger's paddock," Erin spit out like a nail gun. "A mutt of a pony like Cocoa Crème doesn't fit Mr. Dunhill's breeding program. The owner was pissed."

She stared at me, eyes narrowed, voice full of spite. "Mr. Dunhill wanted her gone and he wanted you hired. I heard them."

This was not good. Erin may not know exactly who I was, but if she repeated this information, it could make my job harder. Alan's cover was tight enough, should anyone want to check on it, but I was fast learning that there was as much politicking done in the stable yard as in the country club. I needed to earn the grooms' confidence to get my job done. And if the Horse Ripper was already here hiding in plain sight, maneuvering for a chance to strike, I needed to get that job done fast.

"I had nothing to do with Mandy's firing, Erin. If you hadn't noticed, I'm skating on thin ice, too. Hind's riding me harder than a nag. But beating me up isn't going to change the fact that Mandy's gone and that she isn't coming back."

I released my hold on her T-shirt and we both scrambled to our feet.

"She was my friend."

And that somehow made sense. I'd have beaten up anyone who'd have tried to hurt Nat. "Yeah, well you picked the wrong stooge. Who's been lusting after Ross Hardel?"

Erin blinked at me.

"Katelyn, that's who. Why didn't you beat her up?"

Erin crooked a shy smile. "Who says I didn't?"

The list of suspects kept getting longer. Hiding in this soap opera was far easier for the Horse Ripper than flushing him out was going to be for me.

By ten that night, the house was dark and everyone was in bed. I set my phone on computer mode and entered the names of my fellow grooms and as many riders as I could remember, reporting impressions and all the details I'd learned and asking for as much information on everyone as Alan could dig up. Reluctantly I included a synopsis of the fight with Erin

in the basement. Renee needed to be aware that someone had overheard Mr. Dunhill make Hind hire Ally.

A couple of aspirins and a shower eased some of
my aches. I stowed my workout leg under the bed,
then as I massaged the swollen skin over my residual limb, I dialed Alan's number.

"I'm sorry to call so late," I said after he answered.

"You're not disturbing me. I am, unfortunately, at
home. Alone."

"I need some information that can't wait until tomorrow. Do you have access to a computer?"

"Darling, do you even have to ask?"

Fashion plate notwithstanding, Alan was still a
tech nerd. "Has anyone looked at the win statistics
since the Horse Ripper started his crime spree?"

"Of course. Since the Ripper, the Hardels have
placed in the top three at most of the Grand Prix."

That went to motive. "Did anyone look for a
correlation?"

"All circumstantial, darling. No one wants to
touch it with a ten-foot pole. Not without hard facts.
Especially since they won almost as often before.
Nobody wants egg on their face."

No, not with such big names involved. "It makes
no sense, then, that the Hardels would be the ones
wanting the competition dead."

"They've been scrutinized pretty thoroughly."

"What about Leah Siegel? How did she place?"

"She was out for a chunk of the season with a back

injury. She's just getting her stride back now. The Metropolitan show will be her first Grand Prix since last December."

"No foul play involved with her injury?"

"No, not the Ripper's work. She fell while ice skating and broke a couple of bones."

I leaned against the wall, resting my abused residual limb. "Okay, so when you look at the list of the horses that have died, what comes up as a common denominator?"

"Pharmaceutical agents. And one fire. But there's a rumor that the fire might have been insurance fraud."

My head was starting to pound. "Hardel Industries deals with biotech. No drugs there."

"Ah, but that's where you're wrong. Hardel Industries purchased VetTech, a pharmaceutical company based out of Florida, last spring. When they announced a major research project combining pharmaceuticals with proprietary Hardel nanobiotechnology, the price of their stock shot up."

"So there's a lot of money at stake."

"And money makes the world go round," Alan agreed. "Every time either brother wins, the company gets publicity and a chance to remind everyone of their cutting-edge research. Their web site boasts that they're set to unveil a major innovation."

"When?"

"Sometime in June, according to the web site,"

Alan said. "They say it's going to change the world as we know it."

"Yeah, that's what they said about the Segway, too, and nothing really happened. Do you think there's anything to the claim?"

"I'll see what I can find out, darling."

I chewed my bottom lip. "Does VetTech carry the drugs involved in the horse incidents?"

"If they don't, they could order them without arousing too much suspicion if they did it through their research lab."

"Any way we can check into that? Or if either brother paid the lab a visit?"

"I'll see what I can do."

"Hey, did Renee arrange for a groom named Mandy to get fired?" Somehow I doubted she'd go as far as ruin the poor girl's reputation just to place an agent into the stable.

"No, Patrick Dunhill was willing to work with her if it meant protecting his clients and catching the Horse Ripper."

"Someone else arranged for her to get fired then." And I didn't like that implication. "I think the Ripper might already be here. Can you find out where Mandy is now? She might be angry enough to want to hurt someone."

Alan paused as if digesting the news. "Be careful, darling."

After signing off, I set the phone on its cradle,

ready for Hal's 2 a.m. pickup. To the sound of Dawn's snores on one side, Erin's whimpers on the other and skittering mice feet in the ceiling, I fell into the stiff sheets of my bed.

I hated it here. Hated the way I was being treated. Hated the thankless work and never-ending list of chores everyone else seemed to be able to get through with ease. Every screaming muscle stirred up feelings of failure, and tears dammed in my eyes, ready to soak my pillow. What if Renee was right to doubt I could do this?

I reached for my purse. The silver cigarette case I'd carried with me since the day I'd left the hospital after the accident that severed my leg winked in the moonlight. I popped it open, but couldn't really see the half-smoked cigarette lying there and wished that Nat were here. She would come up with a conspiracy theory as outrageous as the nightly movies she was addicted to and lighten my mood. I smiled, then frowned.

Nat could never know what I did for the Gotham Rose Club. No one could, or I risked putting them and my family in danger from those who would rather the covert portion of the Gotham Rose Club didn't exist.

I shoved the case back in my purse, turned over again and punched my limp pillow.

I had a job to do. I was trained for it. I would do it.

The alarm shrilled much too early. Head pounding from fatigue, eyes burning and stiff muscles screaming for mercy, I dragged myself to the stables with the rest of the crew at the first pink flare of dawn. Hind hovered over me, hoping, I suspected, to catch me doing something wrong. I concentrated on not screwing up my chores and studied the people who came and went through the stables, storing details for Alan to analyze.

If the Horse Ripper was an insider, I had to find a way to blow *his* cover. Or hers. Given the gender disproportion at most stables, a her was just as likely.

At eight, like a double vision, Ross and Roman Hardel strode in tandem into the stable, arguing as their matching sets of long legs ate the ground with power and grace to the tack room. Sex appeal on legs. I'd like to deny it wasn't there, but an active volcano was hard to ignore. I may be dressed down, but I wasn't dead.

Although they were supposed to be identical twins, to me, Ross and Roman looked nothing alike. Ross bubbled with energy like a glass of Cristal, and Roman came across more like flat beer.

Shamelessly I moved my work so I could overhear their discussion.

Their voices were similar, but telling them apart wasn't hard. Roman's was dark gloom and Ross's a rolling, rich timbre that, to my surprise, made me want to sigh.

"I have as much right to be there as you do," Roman said, irritation spiking his voice. "It's my business, too."

"You've never shown an interest before. This is my baby. I don't want to share."

"No, you never do, but you expect me to. I'm not covering your ass anymore."

Ross laughed. "Yeah, that's going to hurt you more than it's going to hurt me."

"You can't keep me out."

"If you're really interested in being part of the project, start at the bottom like I did." The flat tone of authority put an end to the conversation.

"This isn't over."

Before I could quite get out of the way, Roman bowled out of the tack room and practically mowed me over.

He snapped his fingers in my face. I hated it when people did that and backed away automatically. Knee-jerk reaction. Since my accident, my personal bubble of space tended to be larger than most people's. He noticed, of course, and glowered at me. "You're the new groom?"

"That's me."

"Saddle up Trademark," he all but snarled. "Have him ready to go in five minutes."

He pivoted on his heel and headed for the lounge.

"You were eavesdropping."

At the sound of Ross's voice, I swiveled around. The blue of his eyes was so intense I thought I'd catch fire.

"I'm busy working." I stepped past him and grabbed Trademark's bridle, saddle and brush caddy.

"If you want a private conversation, you should think about not shouting or doing it in a public place."

As I started toward Trademark's stall, Ross caught my elbow and smoothly turned me around.

"You look familiar."

I certainly hoped not. "It's really a bad sign when partying starts to affect your memory. You met me yesterday. I'm your new groom, Ally."

His lips quirked as if he were fighting a smile. "I can't place you. Yet."

Ten years ago he hadn't given me a second look. He couldn't remember me from then and we didn't really run in the same circles. My lifestyle, I hated to admit, was much tamer than his. "Somehow I doubt they'd let a groom into the country club."

"I'll figure it out."

Damn his eyes. They were too sharp, too intelligent. He looked as if he could see past the frizzy hair, ragged nails and cheap clothes. The vain part of me wanted to let him know what he saw was just a disguise. The agent part prayed he wouldn't figure out my real identity until the show was over and both Firewall and Waldo were safe.

Instead of moving on to his own business, he followed me into mine and leaned his broad shoulders against the wall as I got Trademark brushed and saddled. He stared at me not like some mild-mannered zoo cheetah, but like one that was hungry and sizing up a prey.

"Are you sure you've done this before?" he asked as I struggled with Trademark's figure-eight noseband. Neither of my horses used one.

"You're making me nervous, staring at me like that. Haven't you ever wanted to do everything right on a new job?" I hit the side of my head with the heel of my hand. "Of course, not. What was I thinking? You don't have a job. You get people like me to do the dirty work."

He peeled himself off the wall and pressed the front of his body against my back. His arms were living steel over mine as he fixed my mistake. I didn't like him this close or the way the heat of his body seeped into mine, causing a finger-in-the-socket jolt to temporarily short-circuit my brain. He'd done this on purpose, the jerk. I wasn't going to give him the satisfaction of letting him know he'd gotten to me. "I'm not going to take over where Mandy left off."

"You want me. You don't like it, but you want me." His voice was as smoldering as sex, and I so didn't want to fall for him.

I slipped past him, using Trademark as a barrier, feeling as if I'd just survived a close call. "Boy, that's a big ego you're packing. Careful not to trip on it. Can I get back to work now? I'm bored and your brother's waiting for his horse."

"Bored, uh." He cupped my chin with a big hand and lightly traced my lips with his thumb. I pulled back at the prickle of static and he laughed. "When you're through with Trademark, saddle up Firewall and Bandit."

"Which one do you want first?" Trademark's hooves clopped on the concrete as we headed toward the arena.

"Both. You're riding Bandit."

I skidded to a halt. Trademark showed his displeasure by pawing at the ground. "What?"

"I've already cleared it with Hind."

"But—"

He cocked his head, assessing me. "You know how to ride, don't you?"

"Yes, but—"

"Then stop sputtering and get going. I have a meeting in an hour." His face turned serious. "We need to talk. Hind might have hired you, but you're working for me."

Chapter 5

I managed to throw my leg over the saddle without catching the prosthesis and embarrassing myself, even with Ross watching me like some sort of scientific specimen.

I needed to ride. Riding helped rid me of the caustic poison that stress built up. And I'd racked up enough stress for a month these past couple of days.

Spokes of sunlight gleamed through the foliage and gilded the morning as Ross led the horses onto a woodsy trail. The pines and maples and oaks seemed to weave their branches and close out the world. I filled my lungs with crisp air, exhaling the soot of tension with every breath.

When we reached the river trail, Ross glanced at me over his shoulder. Challenge flashed in his eyes. "Ready for a run?"

"I'm right with you."

As I gathered the reins, Bandit snorted in anticipation. His haunches bunched with power. His hooves struck the soft ground with the rhythmic *ta-da-dum* of his canter, starting an internal music that set my body and soul singing. My seat deepened and molded around his dark-brown back and I gave in to the sheer pleasure of riding.

Well, mostly.

I mean, Ross was right there beside me, too big to ignore, making me mad enough to fire up my competitive side.

Geek-boy's seat had improved in the past ten years. His legs were steady. His hands were calm and soft. His body rocked perfectly to the rhythm of Firewall's movements, streaking a bolt of electricity straight through me.

Definitely do not *go there.*

There was an energy about him that pulled me to him in spite of myself. I didn't like the way it made me squirm as if I was that desperate sixteen-year-old longing for someone, anyone, to find me pretty, knowing that red scar below my right knee would never do anything but turn stomachs.

I must have groaned out loud because Ross shot

me a questioning look. Face flaming, I nudged Bandit faster and raced past him.

At the top of a hill, Ross slowed Firewall back to a walk. I rode alongside, our knees bumping intimately. His gaze held a mixture of surprise and admiration. "You can ride."

As if a groom couldn't possibly ride well. I don't know why, but his attitude nettled me. "Why yes, I ride at my country estate when I can tear myself away from my New York City penthouse. I meet the ladies at the club once a week for tea, and I sit around pampering myself the rest of the time. When I'm not jetting around the world on vacation, of course. Oh, if I just had the time, I'd be an Olympic hopeful, too. But you know how it is. All those charity parties."

He held both hands up in surrender. "I meant it as a compliment." Shaking his head, he added, "You sounded just like Claudine. Spooky."

"You wanted to talk," I snapped. "So talk."

His jaw tightened and his face turned grim. "I've had you checked out."

"Gee, thanks for the vote of confidence."

"Standard procedure."

I frowned. "Not for me."

"You're clean." As if his gaze had lie detecting abilities, he pierced me with it. "Too clean."

"I'll work on a felony or two."

His mouth thinned. "You're a pain, you know that?"

"You're not exactly Mr. Personality, either."

He lifted one eyebrow. I guess not too many women had told him he wasn't Mr. Wonderful.

"Have you heard of the Horse Ripper?" he asked.

"Who hasn't? Everyone's buzzing about him."

"Then you're probably aware that Firewall could be the next victim."

I nodded. "Him and Waldo. I'm keeping my eyes open. I don't want some sicko hurting the horses."

His gaze narrowed. "I don't believe in coincidence. Mandy leaving and you taking her place right before the show."

I gasped at his insinuation. "You're not thinking I'm the Ripper!"

Only the hollow knocking of a woodpecker deep in the woods broke his stony silence. I sensed I was very much on trial here.

"Look," I said, exasperated. I mean, really, I was here to protect *him*. "I don't know what happened to Mandy, but I can assure you I had nothing to do with her leaving." Not directly anyway. "My only interest is doing my job. I'm on probation right now and I don't want to blow it. I *need* this job. *I* don't have the luxury of a trust fund. I was assigned to your horses by the luck of the draw. I know what I'm doing." Mostly.

"Patrick Dunhill specifically asked you be given both Waldo and Roman's and my horses."

I shrugged, switching the tail of my reins to the other side of Bandit's neck. "My former boss knows him and she gave me a reference. No strong-arming involved. If you're not happy with my work, ask for another groom. You've got more pull with Mr. Dunhill than I'll ever have." That would make my job harder, but not impossible.

"I'm just saying I'm keeping my eye on you."

"Oh, goody."

For a minute all I could hear was the muted footfalls of the horses as we entered a large hay field. "He's going to go after Magnus," Ross said.

"Magnus? What makes you think so? Magnus hasn't even entered a show. At least I've never heard of him. Besides, the Ripper goes after horses who've won Grand Prix."

His mouth became a flat line. "Magnus's performance is going to make headlines."

"If you say so." Was this wishful thinking on Ross's part? Something about his certainty set off alarms, but I didn't know where the fire was. I just smelled the smoke.

He didn't take his gaze off my face, which was starting to make me nervous. "I say so. And I'm trusting you with my horses." He made it sound like a big deal.

Ross suddenly drew Firewall to a halt and swiveled to look around.

From the woods came a buzzing like a giant mosquito.

A red dirt bike shot out from the trees to our left. To keep Bandit from spooking, I turned him to face the threat. Pricking his ears forward and back, he hunched down, ready to flee. His heart beat a frightened storm against my thighs as the bike zipped over the ground toward us, spewing dirt and grass.

"It's okay, boy." I rubbed a comforting hand up and down his neck. "What's that jerk doing? Can't he see us?"

"Hey!" Ross waved one arm to draw the biker's attention. He ignored him, bent his black-helmeted head farther down on the handlebar and charged straight at Bandit's side. My fists choked the reins. "The idiot's not going to stop."

"Get back to the stable," Ross ordered, placing Firewall between me and the biker, offering me a route of escape.

"Firewall's too valuable—"

"Go! Now."

I hesitated, weighing Ross's trust against what I could do to help him, then I spun Bandit a quarter turn and urged him into a gallop. Getting help took top priority. My pulse rocketed to the drumbeat of Bandit's hooves. The biker changed course and revved his engine for pursuit. Ross tried to cut him off. Firewall reared, nearly unseating him and giving the biker the opportunity to zip by.

"Come on, boy." Bandit, propelled by adrenaline, gave his all, but it wasn't going to be enough.

The dirt bike outraced Firewall and drew alongside Bandit, its motor a growl, its exhaust a hot stink that wrapped around my left leg. Bandit sidestepped away from the noisy monster. I lost my right stirrup and couldn't feel it to regain my anchor, putting my balance in jeopardy.

"Whoooaah," I encouraged, hanging on to my seat with sheer determination.

Laughing like a maniac, he took another swipe at us. Ross was catching up.

"Get lost," I yelled to the biker. Furious, I kicked at him. "Back off!"

Out in the open, I couldn't outrun him and I didn't want the biker to turn on Firewall. I reached down and shoved the stirrup back onto my foot, then drove Bandit toward the cover of the woods. Ross was gaining ground.

The biker's narrower frame allowed him more mobility on the uneven ground and around the trees. Sweat foamed on Bandit's shoulders and peeled off in ribbons. He was tiring fast.

"Hang on, boy," I said in between puffing breaths. "I'll get you home."

My one chance to stop this jerk was to unseat him. I urged Bandit into the cross-country field.

With sure calculation, I aimed for the flattest part of the clearing. I slowed Bandit's gallop to a canter so I could balance myself. The biker zipped out of the woods from between two trees and drew dangerously close to Bandit's left flank. Ross shot out of the woods and cut a sharp angle to cut off the biker.

I couldn't allow Ross to risk Firewall. I sat the canter, gathering its energy. The biker drew parallel to us. Letting go of both stirrups, I swung my legs forward to gain momentum. Then, holding on to the saddle's pommel, I reversed direction and swung my legs back, extending them above Bandit's rump. At the height of the apex, I cocked my hips. My breath whooshed from my lungs as the full weight of both legs hammered the biker, toppling him and his steel horse.

Never letting go of the pommel, I planted both feet together on the ground and sprang up. I wasn't going to win any points for style, but my right leg cleared Bandit's hips. I landed astride the saddle and fumbled for the stirrups.

I glanced over my shoulder. The rider was pinned under his bike, but moving. Like a cheetah built for speed and lean strength, Ross leaped onto the biker as he righted his bike. They rolled on the ground until Ross came up on top. With a swift move, Ross cut the bike's engine. A panting Firewall trotted toward me.

I vaulted off Bandit. Ignoring the jar to my residual limb, I grabbed Firewall's reins and held on to both horses.

Ross ripped off the biker's helmet. The kid couldn't be more than fifteen.

"What kind of jackass mows a horse down with a bike?" Ross said between clenched teeth, each word as biting as a bullet. He grabbed two fistfuls of the kid's jacket.

"Don't hit me, please don't hit me." Arm protecting his head, the biker struggled to escape Ross's unyielding grip. "It was a joke."

"Nobody's laughing. These are champion show horses and this is private property."

The biker's face scrunched up as if insulted. "Then why'd you give me a hundred bucks to spook the brown horse?"

Ross's whole body stiffened. "When?"

"As if you don't know."

"Answer the question." His voice had no give.

The kid swallowed hard and shook like an aspen. "At the gas station an hour ago."

Right before Ross and Roman had shown up at the stable. The sweat running down my back turned ice-cold. Ross had insisted we go riding. He'd insisted I ride Bandit. And now this guy was saying Ross had paid him to hurt me. "You paid this jerk to hurt me?"

"Don't be an idiot. Even if I was going to wring your neck, I wouldn't risk hurting a horse." Ross got in the kid's face. "Was the guy wearing a black polo shirt?"

I gasped. Roman. Ross thought Roman had done this.

The kid squinted as if in pain. "I—I can't remember."

Jaw set, Ross glared at me. "Ride to the stable and call the cops."

Roman wanting to hurt me made no more sense than Ross wanting to hurt me. "What about Firewall?"

"Leave him."

* * *

The cops took my statement in Hind's office while Hind scowled in the background. Ross and Roman glared at each other across Hind's desk.

"Why would I pay someone to hurt my horse?" Roman practically spat.

"To make me look like the bad guy," Ross said. "You've been jabbing at me for months because I won't give you a slice of my project."

"You think too much of yourself," Roman scoffed. "If I wanted to hurt you, I'd have gone after Firewall, not Bandit."

"Smokescreen. You're good at that."

Roman tossed up his hands. "There's just no winning with you." He turned to the kid. "Did I pay you?"

The kid's gaze bounced from brother to brother. "One of you did." He shoved a hand into an inside pocket of his jacket and pulled out a wad of twenties as proof.

"And you didn't think there was anything wrong with that?" Ross said so softly that the rumble of anger took a few seconds to catch up.

The kid was sweating as if he was in a sauna. "All I know is that some guy gave me this money to spook the brown horse. I wasn't going to hurt him, so I didn't see the harm in making a few easy bucks."

The cops put an end to the argument by cuffing the kid and stuffing him in the back of their cruiser.

Ross and Roman, both their faces set like stones, followed them to the police station.

And things at the stable went back to normal.

Except for my thoughts. A jumble of questions trotted in my mind with no answers shaking loose. Made me wish Alan had some truth serum I could pour in Ross's coffee next time we had a chat. I couldn't decide if someone had played him or if he'd played me.

Needing distraction, I approached Leah Siegel just before lunch, taking the opportunity of the lull to introduce myself to her.

She was an overly polite and shy twenty-something whose pale features and willowy figure made her seem to practically disappear in the woodwork.

"Is there anything I can do for you before I take my break?" I asked, resting my weight on the stall door to ease the load off my prosthesis. I'd need a thicker stump sock if I was going to make it through the week without damaging the skin over my residual limb.

"There is one thing," she said, brushing short, buffed nails through the ends of her long strawberry-blond ponytail. "Would you mind seeing if you can find another salt lick for Waldo?"

"No problem."

She played with Waldo's mane while he munched on hay. "I hear there was an incident this morning."

"A kid on a dirt bike tried to spook the Hardel horses."

She seemed relieved. "So it's not the Horse Ripper, then?"

Hard to say who'd set up the kid, but Leah looked as if she needed reassurance, not suppositions. "Doesn't look like it."

"With this being Waldo's first show of the season, I've been worried about the Ripper striking up here."

"Do you have any idea who'd want to hurt Waldo?"

"None." She shook her head. "That's just it. It's so senseless. I mean. It's not like it would do anyone any good. You can't kill too much of the competition before it becomes obvious who did it."

Good point. One of those cold shivers of realization snaked down my spine. What if there was one specific target? And what if all the killings were to mask that one specific death? Magnus. Ross had been so sure that Magnus was next on the Ripper's list. Was there more to his concern than he was letting on? Or was he just an overprotective owner? "Nobody said criminals were smart."

Leah rubbed Waldo's cheek. "In the meantime we all fear for our horses."

"I can assure you that nothing's going to happen to Waldo. Not on my watch."

She smiled and it brightened her face. "That makes me feel better."

"I'll go round up that salt lick for you."

"Thank you. I appreciate it." Her genuine appreciation widened her smile, and she returned to spoiling her gelding.

As I neared the tack room on my way to the feed room, the sound of a raised voice caught my attention. Claudine Breitbach, Roman Hardel's girlfriend—stinking of Opium perfume and dressed in Hermes breeches and a Romfh practice polo—stooped over the smaller-statured Erin like a vulture over carrion. Her Bergdorf-blond hair was caught at the nape in a velvet ribbon the same Wedgwood-blue as her shirt. The loose hair below the ribbon spilled into a ponytail of ringlets too symmetrical to be natural. I should know.

"You call this clean?" Claudine waved a bridle in front of Erin's face, making the groom flinch.

"No, ma'am."

"The leather's so dry it's a hazard." Claudine yanked on one rein so hard that it snapped. "That's coming out of your paycheck. Do you understand?"

Erin's eyes narrowed, the green of her irises growing rime. "Yes, ma'am."

Claudine launched the bridle at Erin who barely caught it in time. "And this—" Claudine pulled a breastplate from the top of a saddle "—is crusted with sweat. That could cause a sore. There's a show in a week. How's Cause Célèbre supposed to shine with a big sore on his chest?"

"I don't know, ma'am."

"'I don't know, ma'am,'" Claudine mimicked. "It

doesn't take a genius to figure it out, you imbecile. Clean the damn tack every day. That's what you're paid to do."

"Yes, ma'am." Erin reached for the breastplate.

Claudine hurled it in Erin's direction. One of the straps whipped around, lashing Erin's cheek and causing a welt.

"And I want my watch back."

Erin frowned, shaking her head in rapid strokes. "I don't know where it is, ma'am."

"Of course you do. You saw me put it in my locker. I saw you staring at it. It's a Movado. That's going to take a long time to pay back on your salary."

"I didn't—"

"Don't you talk back at me!" Claudine raised a hand above her head, gritting her teeth as if she was putting everything she had behind the blow. I stepped in, catching the downward projectile of her fist in my palm and squeezing until I could feel the bones of her fingers on the edge of snapping.

"I wouldn't," I said. "No unless you want to be charged with assault."

Claudine curled back her glossy top lip like a dog. "Who do you think you are? I'm going to have that bitch charged with theft and you with assault."

"I wouldn't." I nodded toward the security camera pointing almost directly at us. "Not unless you want that tape showing up on a segment of *Lives of the Rich & Nasty*." The new show on Fox had celebrities fear-ing for their reputations every time they went out. Many of Hollywood's A-list and society's best-known faces had appeared in less than favorable light—their fits of temper no doubt provoked by persistent paparazzi bent on obtaining film footage and fat paychecks. I didn't quite understand people's love-hate fascination with celebrities. "I'm sure the local police would also be delighted to receive a copy."

"Ally, don't," Erin said, her voice trembling. "It's okay. I can handle it."

"Ms. Breitbach is sorry she overreacted and is ready to apologize." With a look, I dared Claudine to defy me. I'd put together enough charity events to match tempers with the most impatient of florists and the most testy of chefs. Compared to them, Claudine was sponge cake.

"I'm sorry, Erin," Claudine said between clenched teeth. The brittle blue of her eyes reflected the cold sharpness of promised revenge.

I hoped Renee's in with Patrick Dunhill was good. I probably shouldn't have jumped in and stuck my nose in business that wasn't mine. But people like Claudine tended to rub me the wrong way, undercover or not.

Erin simply nodded, eyes wide, as if she feared reprisal. "I'll get the tack cleaned and keep an eye open for your watch."

"I appreciate that."

Erin's gaze jumped from me to Claudine and back, then she slinked out of the tack room.

"You want to piss on someone," I said, squeezing a bit harder on the fist still prisoner in my grip, "you'd better do it on me and not Erin or you'll regret the day you picked on her. Is that understood?"

Claudine smiled with a malevolent twitch. If looks could kill, hers would have shot me clean through the forehead. "You bet your sweet ass, darling. You have *no* idea who you're dealing with."

"Ill-mannered white trash posing as society cream. Erin works twelve hours a day for less-than-minimum wage to keep you and your horse happy. The least you could do is show your appreciation."

"You'd better pack your bags, because you're going to be out on your ass before the end of the day."

I imitated Renee's cryptic smile and released Claudine's hand. "We'll see."

I left Claudine stewing and tracked down a salt lick for Waldo.

"Here you go," I said, and slipped the pink brick of salt in the holder in Waldo's stall.

"Thank you so much."

Claudine could definitely take manner lessons from Leah.

Erin grabbed me as I went by the cross ties where she was tacking up Cause Célèbre.

"I, uh," she said, looking up and down the aisle to make sure neither Hind nor Claudine were nearby. "Thanks for sticking up for me."

"What are friends for?"

"Claudine's been riding me like a witch on a broom lately. I can't do anything right for her."

"You can't let her treat you that way. And her threatening to garnish your pay is pure bull. New reins and a new watch are pocket change for her."

Erin's brow furrowed, giving her that iguana look I'd come to associate with her. "I like my job. I don't want to get fired."

"Even if you did, a hard worker like you could get another job, no problem." I could think of a dozen stables I could put in a word for her.

She pursed her lips and shook her head. "I need to be here."

Need? Disturbing word choice. "Why?"

She flipped her braid back and shrugged. "Just because."

Hind's irritating whistle rent the air. "You!" he said pointing at me. "Get Azur ready for the trainer. And you." He crooked a finger at Erin. "Get in my office."

Erin gulped as she closed the stall door.

"You'll be okay."

She nodded, but I saw wetness gathering in her eyes.

Keeping an eye on the time, I got Azur ready for her training session with Grant Montney and headed toward the arena a few minutes early.

There was something about the cantering strike of hooves against the deep arena footing that sounded like a heartbeat. I'd always found the rhythm sooth-

ing. The look on both Juliane's, one of the youngest
riders in contention for the Grand Prix, and Claudine's faces said neither of them did. Grant Montney,
standing in the center of the ring, surrounded by two
gymnastic grids of jumps, was using a mixture of en-
couragement, pleading and unbending authority to
get what he needed out of his students.

Practice the week before a big show was a serious thing.

"Okay, Claudine," Grant said, after a heart-to-
heart talk with Juliane, who seemed to be wiping
tears with the back of her gloved hand. "Your turn."

Claudine cued her horse, Cause Célèbre, a bay
with an attitude as cantankerous as his owner's. He
gave a little buck, unbalancing Claudine's seat, then
jumped ahead too fast. She manhandled him toward
the first fence, two crossed poles.

"Keep your weight down through your leg," Grant
reminded her from the center of the ring. "You have
a tendency to raise your heels when your horse takes
off. That's going to land you on your face one of
these days."

She bounced to the second jump, a straight vertical.

"Look toward the end of the grid."

One stride to the square oxer, a spread fence using two sets of standards and poles.

"Keep him straight. Come on, Claudine. Left leg.
Left leg. Keep him straight."

Her gelding raised his head, showing the whites

of his eyes as they approached the ascending oxer, a sloping spread jump.

"Lighten your contact," Grant said. "You're hurting his mouth."

"He's going to run out," Claudine said.

"Not if you keep him between your legs."

The gelding dropped a back foot as he went over the spread. The far pole bounced in the jump cups, but stayed up.

Claudine spurred her horse to the vertical plank that looked more solid than it was. The gelding started fighting her, nostrils flaring, legs pistoning almost in place as if he wanted nothing better than to shake off his rider. He popped over the plank at the last second, making for a less-than-graceful effort that smacked Claudine around like a rag doll. Secretly I cheered.

"Keep your stride steady," Grant said. "Don't let him set the pace. Two strides. Not five. You took off too close."

She jerked her horse in the mouth to stop him, then sawed on the reins. "He's not listening."

"Then you're not speaking to him right." Grant grabbed her boot and practically yanked her off the saddle. "I see you pull on his mouth like that one more time and you can look for another trainer. That horse is your partner, not your slave."

He sent her to the other end of the arena to practice a figure eight fence to calm both her and the horse down.

Juliane had a go at the same exercise. With all the pressure stable gossip said she got from her parents, the kid was like an elastic band stretched too tight. She overrode her more-than-willing horse and knocked down the last fence.

"Try again," Grant encouraged.

Juliane moved into position, trotting over the cross pole, then jumping the first vertical and oxer. She pushed her horse too hard toward the second oxer and he slammed on the brakes, crashing into the fence. She burst into tears. "I can't do this!"

"Yes, you can," Grant insisted.

But Juliane wasn't listening. She took off for the gate, vaulted off and handed me her horse while she stormed away, boots stomping on the concrete aisle. Her mother shot up from the viewing stand and pushed her way into the arena, arms pumping, driving straight at Grant.

"Hey," I said to Juliane, trying to control both the frightened Loophole and the curious Azur who wanted a closer inspection of the chestnut gelding. "I'm already holding a horse."

Juliane was crying too hard to hear—or care. Her mother's voice echoed in the cavernous ring as she blistered Grant with a piece of her mind. Every parent thought their child was the next Olympic star.

"The lid come off the pressure cooker?" Katelyn asked, nodding in the direction Juliane had disappeared.

"You could say that," I said, handing her Loophole's reins. "Juliane needs a vacation without a horse in sight."

"Not likely to happen as long as Mom's in charge."

I'd spent enough time adding suspects to my list. It was time to start eliminating. The master key I'd swiped from Hind's desk was burning a hole in my pocket. Tonight I'd make time to use it.

Chapter 6

That night I spent several hours studying the security guard's circuit around the farm. When I was sure everyone was asleep, I eased the screen off the window and shimmied onto the roof of the porch. From there I slipped over the side, good foot reaching for the railing. Once I felt solid wood under my foot, let go of the eaves, then jumped onto the soft ground.

The moon played hide-and-seek with the clouds, creating darting shadows that had my heart jumping and my mind imagining skulking bogeymen at every turn. I hugged the tree line and made my way to the stables, keeping an eye out for movement. I figured I had about forty minutes to snoop inside the owners' lockers before the security guard's patrol brought him back to the stable.

Once inside, a few nickers greeted me and curious equine eyes followed my trek down the aisle to the tack room. I was aware of every creak of the rafters and of every spike of pulse beating against my neck. Did any of the other Gotham Rose agents feel as nervous as I did while spying?

Now's not the time for comparison, Alexa. Do your job!

Drying my sweaty palms against the front of my jeans, I blew out a breath, then I reached for the master key in my pocket. That's when I noticed the faint glow of light coming from the direction of the indoor arena. I frowned. That wasn't right. No one was supposed to be here this late. Why wasn't the guard investigating this obvious breach of security?

Hackles firing a mad warning up and down my neck, I pressed close to the shadows stretching from the stall walls and crept up the aisle in the silent toe-first step Jimmy had taught us.

As I neared the arena, the even rhythm of a muffled canter pumped the ragged beat of my heart. Who was riding this late?

I peered around the corner. Only one of the six banks of lights was turned on. Whoever was riding was using only the top half of the arena. I'd have to get closer.

Crouching, I inched my way to the arena door. I

eased my head around in time to have horse legs pound right by me. Holding my breath, I poked my head through the gate. With a jolt, I realized I was looking at Magnus and Ross. They popped over the same grid that had given Juliane and Claudine such a fit. The black horse floated over the obstacles in a perfect bascule with air to spare. All muscle and sinew and concentration. Man and horse made the exercise look too easy.

I watched as they sailed over the combinations in perfect unison. Ross was right. Magnus looked like a strong contender for the upcoming Grand Prix. But why keep the horse under wraps? Because he was afraid the Horse Ripper would go after him. Had the Ripper struck Magnus once already? I'd have to ask Alan.

Something about this late-night ride just didn't feel right.

Ross brought Magnus down to a walk, loosened the reins and patted the horse's neck as he cooled him. "Good job, boy. I wish you could talk and let me know how that all felt."

Magnus snorted and stretched his neck down.

"Yeah, I imagine that feels pretty good, considering."

Considering what? But Ross didn't expound.

As he hopped off Magnus and started leading him back into the stable, I quickly made my way back up the aisle. From the shadows of Hind's office, I watched as Ross bathed, dried and brushed Magnus—doing all the scut work usually left to the grooms. He moved with the smooth grace of someone comfortable with himself and his body, of someone in complete control of his universe. His tender smile as he praised the horse and gently stroked his muzzle was enough to steal my breath. He'd probably blush if he knew I'd witnessed this unmanly show of affection, and that brought a certain satisfaction.

My heart thumped hard in my chest as Ross strode by. I hunkered down deeper in the office. He came out of the tack room with a spray bottle filled with a dark liquid that he sprayed all over the horse, working it carefully into the coat. What in the world was he doing?

Magnus flattened his ears, flicked his tail and stomped one foot to show he wasn't enjoying the process. When Ross was done, Magnus looked brighter. Some sort of coat conditioner? I had to find out.

After Ross left, I stole to the tack room, unhooked the security camera as Alan had showed me. I turned on my Maglite and spotted Ross's locker. Using the master key, I opened it.

The inside was plastered with training schedules, complete with colors and graphs. A leather jacket and training chaps hung from a hook. The plastic bottle with the dark liquid was parked between a pair of dusty boots. I picked up the bottle, shook it and sniffed it, but couldn't tell what was in it. I couldn't take the whole bottle or Ross would grow suspicious and I needed his trust. I looked around for a container and found a syringe in the first-aid kit.

Just as I was sucking up the sample, steady footsteps echoed on the concrete aisle. Crap. He was coming back.

I hurried my sample snatching, capped the bottle and stuffed it back in its place. I pocketed the syringe while I searched for a hiding place. He was too close for me to zip out unnoticed. The utility counter was too open. I aimed the key at another locker, but my hand was shaking too much to make the connection. The boots were right at the door. With no other choice, I eased myself into Ross's locker and closed the door just as the tack room door opened.

His leather jacket, hanging there, molded around me like arms. His scent, like a freshly cleaned saddle and something musky, flirted with me. I could almost hear his teasing laughter. "My, my, Ally Cross in my arms. Guess you're more interested than I thought."

I was *not*.

I flicked the offending arm of the jacket off my shoulder.

The tight slats on the small vent of the locker door made it hard to see out, even with the lights suddenly blazing through the room.

He walked right by his locker, making my heart somersault. He picked up the first-aid kit and looked at it quizzically, then grabbed a stack of papers from the top of the utility counter and started shuffling them until he found the one he wanted.

My nose prickled from the battling scents inside the locker. The urge to sneeze built pressure against my eyeballs until they teared. I wrinkled my nose, trying to contain the sneeze. Holding my breath, I silently prodded Ross to hurry up and leave.

After adding a note to one of the sheets, he stuffed the whole bunch in his back pocket, snapped off the lights and pulled the door shut behind him.

Cupping my hand over my nose, I allowed a tiny *tchoo* to relieve the pressure, then rubbed my nose until the urge for a bigger sneeze disappeared. I eased out of the locker, listened until I heard the growl of Ross's Jaguar recede. Keeping an ear open for Ross and the guard, I made a hurried search of the rest of the lockers, but found nothing I hadn't expected.

Once back in my room, I placed a call to Alan, who didn't sound too pleased at the late-night interruption. "I need to make a dead drop."

"Can it wait till morning?" Hope skimmed through Alan's voice.

"I need to know what the stuff is right away." I needed to understand what Ross was up to.

"I'll send someone out."

"Tell your courier to drive past the front entrance to the far corner of the cross-country field. There's a V-shaped jump made out of stacked creosoted logs.

I'll put the package at the base of the V. The security cameras don't scan that far."

"Check."

I swaddled the syringe in plastic wrap I found in the kitchen and a padded envelope I had in my duffel bag. I made the drop and headed back to the house for a much-needed shower and some sleep. Tomorrow I'd inspect Magnus from the tips of his ears to the bottom of his hooves to see if I could spot anything out of place.

On my way back to the house, as I passed close to the stable, I spotted movement in one of the pools of moonlight dotting the stableyard. Not the slow, bored movements of the guard or Ross's self-assured walk, but stealthy movements—like mine. Whoever was here didn't want to be seen.

Dressed in black from head to toe, a figure skimmed the outer edge of the stable like a snake. Male? Female? I couldn't tell from this far. My heart thumped hard. The Horse Ripper?

I reached for my cell phone and discovered I'd left it in my room. I had no choice but to follow the intruder. I flattened myself against the stable and peered around the corner in time to see the figure slink inside the stable door. Where was the guard?

Barely rolling the door open, I slipped inside. I stood still while my eyes adjusted to the deeper darkness inside. Not a horse called after me. The air crisped with palpable tension. As shapes became visible, I moved silently down the aisle, wishing I was armed with a gun instead of a utility knife.

Each stall with its protective grille appeared like a black hole ready to suck me in. Each snort, each shift of muscle from a horse squirted a shot of adrenaline into my bloodstream. The scent of hay and manure and leather sharpened. My vision narrowed but brightened.

The frightened squeal of a horse, followed by the jiggling of a chain, sent my heart tripping into double time. Somewhere ahead. Which stall?

You have picked the wrong place to hit, I thought, the tightness of anger replacing the twitchiness of fear. I slipped my groom's utility knife out of my back pocket and the Maglite from my waistband. *Had to wait till dark, did you? You're not getting out of here tonight.*

Heart pumping madly, I stopped just before the half-opened stall door and sucked in a breath. Bay Bridge Bandit? Why this horse when his chances of winning were slim?

Clamping my mouth tight so my rapid breaths couldn't warn the intruder, I craned my neck to see inside the stall. The intruder was bent over Bandit's back leg in a way that made me think he was familiar with horses.

The window was barred. The only way out was through me. Balancing on my left foot, I shoved the stall door the rest of the way open with my right and turned on the flashlight. "Drop it!"

For a moment the intruder's rounded back remained frozen in my circle of light. I couldn't see the face, and the bulky jacket hid the shape of the body.

"I said, drop it!"

The flying roundhouse kick caught me in the chest. Air whooshed out of my lungs. I staggered back, caught myself on the edge of the stall door. Bandit neighed in panic. His feet scrambled on the bedding as he tried to evade the fight.

With a guttural cry, the intruder plowed into me, knocking the knife out of my hand. It skittered on the concrete and out of sight. I hung on to the collar of the intruder's jacket, forcing him off balance. He staggered into the stall door, then fell hard onto the concrete aisle.

I aimed the flashlight at his temple. He swung an arm, blocking my hand, and bashed the side of my head with something hard. My grip loosened. He bucked me off.

Behind us, Bandit's panic increased. He leaped forward. Dreading the strike of steel shoes against my skull, I raised one arm to protect my head as he sailed over me. Chain flapping, he took off at a gallop down the concrete aisle.

I lunged after the intruder, catching an ankle and jerking him to the ground. He kicked with his free boot, jamming a heel into my cheekbone. I saw stars, but hung on to his leg. As he lifted his free leg to kick again, I threw myself onto him, catching the fat of his thigh into my shoulder and dulling the force of the blow.

Grunting, he rolled us over and wrapped his fingers around my throat. I lifted my knee toward his groin, gaining a cry of pain. I threw my arms between his and broke his grip, then smashed both his temples with the heels of my hands. Stunned he rolled off me and kept rolling until he was free. He scrambled to his feet and ran.

I jumped to my feet and chased after him. He grabbed halters from the hooks in front of each stall and threw them at me. Batting the flying objects, I kept after him. "Help! Guard! Someone!"

Bandit, trapped by the closed stable door, panicked at the intruder's approach. His feet clattered on the concrete. He reared, forcing the intruder to swerve from his course.

The intruder reached into the area where the cleaning equipment was stashed and stabbed at me with a pitchfork.

Bandit took off for the other end of the stable. I reached for a shovel and rammed at the pitchfork. With a fierce jab, the intruder lunged toward me. He let go of his weapon, then sprinted to the stable door, shoved it open and fled into the stableyard.

I chased after him into the maze of paddocks, but it soon became clear that I couldn't catch him. With my stupid leg, I couldn't run fast enough or far enough on the rough terrain to corner him. Breathing hard, I probed the pastures and found nothing but night staring back at me.

Damn it! I smacked my hated prosthesis against the fence and growled in frustration.

Because of my defect, a possible horse killer had gotten away.

As I made my way back to the stable, I found the guard out cold in the golf cart he used to patrol the grounds. He was still breathing, but had an egg-size knot on the back of his head. I used his cell phone to call the police, paramedics and Hind. Hind would call the vet and the Hardels.

Using my left foot to feel the pedal, I drove the cart back to the stable. The burly guard was moaning back to consciousness.

"Are you okay?" I asked him, looking into his eyes, not quite sure what I was looking for.

"Someone hit me from behind."

"Stay right here. Don't move. The paramedics and police are on their way. I don't want you to pass out again."

He tried to sit up straighter. "Horses—"

"I'm on it."

Hugging the knot on his head with a hand, the guard nodded. I flipped on the stable lights and went looking for Bandit.

I found him standing trembling in his stall, a chain twitch still dangling from his muzzle, the whites of his eyes wide with fear.

As I stood by the open door, crooning to Bandit to calm him, the brass name placard caught my eye. "Firewall."

I frowned. Bandit was in his proper stall. Firewall's was right next to it and he was right where he belonged, too. How had the placards gotten switched? Had the intruder meant to harm Firewall? Ross had been so sure that Magnus was the Horse Ripper's true target.

"Whoooa," I said as I approached Bandit. "It's okay. You're safe now. Nobody's going to hurt you."

Not that I was certain about that. How the hell had the intruder gotten to Bandit so easily? Even with a guard on duty. Even with security cameras. He could have killed a dozen horses before anyone was the wiser. That was unacceptable.

There was going to be hell to pay once Mr. Dunhill and the Hardels heard the news. Would it cost me my job? Getting fired wouldn't put me on Renee's good side.

I put together what I hoped was a viable explanation for my being out this late at night. I'd say I couldn't sleep and went down for a glass of milk when I spotted a light on in the stable. I loosened the twitch, removed it and rubbed the circulation back into the tender skin of Bandit's muzzle. Carefully I looked Bandit over, but found no other mark on him. Maybe I'd been lucky enough to stop the intruder before he could do any damage. But the niggling sense of failure still ate at me.

I'd messed up. Because of my leg.

And for the first time since the accident, I had to admit that I couldn't do everything.

Sirens pierced the quiet of the night. Time to face the music.

Between the police, Hind and the vet, I was answering questions until dawn. My inability to give them helpful details frustrated me as much as it did them. I wanted this intruder caught. Policemen combed the paddocks, but came up with nothing, which didn't help my gloomy mood. And they took the name placards to examine them for prints. Maybe Alan could get a peek at their results.

A headache pounded at my temples like some demented construction worker manning a jackhammer. Bone-deep fatigue and aching muscles made every move a torture. My cheek throbbed from the intruder's blow and was now turning a nasty purple.

The vet okayed my feeding Bandit his morning ration. I spent extra time with him, then did the rest of my morning chores. An examination of Magnus's coat gave me no answer as to what Ross might have rubbed on him last night.

When I returned to check on Bandit, misery stamped his face. The usually greedy gelding hadn't touched his grain and he looked both hot and cold at the same time.

"What's wrong, boy?" I ran a hand over his coat. He flinched as if my touch was painful. When he tried to move, he practically stumbled. I gasped at the sight of his back legs. They were a mess of gaping wounds. Flesh was rotting away, exposing cartilage and tendon. The wounds oozed with pus as if the horse was trying to turn himself inside out.

I yelled for Hind who came running. He swore at the sight. "What did you do?"

"Nothing! The intruder must have gotten to him before I scared him away."

"I don't care who's pulling strings for you," he bellowed. "Since you got here, you've caused nothing but problems. I have a reputation for sterling care. It's taken me two decades to earn it, and you're destroying it in under a week."

"We can argue about sacking me later. Right now Bandit needs help."

Hind stalked away to call the vet once more.

An hour later, I stood at Bandit's head, holding him while the vet bandaged his legs. Roman Hardel marched in, a grim expression etching his face.

"What's going on here?" Roman demanded, fists on his hips like a general facing a lackluster troop. "You said the horse was fine."

The vet, a beanstalk of a guy with thinning blond hair, rose up to meet Roman. "He wasn't showing any signs of distress and it's too early for the blood test results to have come back."

"What's wrong with him?" Roman's gaze flicked to the half-bandaged leg, curled his lip in disgust, then settled back on the vet.

The vet scraped a hand over his face and shook his head. "I've never seen anything like this before."

"Is he going to live?"

The vet frowned. "I can't say for sure, but it looks as if he's been injected with some sort of toxin that's causing necrosis of—"

"Is he going to live?" Roman insisted.

The vet let out a long breath. "If we can stop the toxin's damage, there's a chance we can repair the—"

"But his showing days are over." A flat statement. As if Roman had already decided that was the only outcome.

"I can't say for sure. I need to run some tests and find out what's causing the flesh to die."

"How soon?"

The vet shook his head, confused. "I'm sorry?"

"How soon before you know?"

"I'll expedite, but—"

Roman's forehead pleated like a lampshade. "If you don't have an answer by tonight, I want him put out of his misery."

I must have gasped because Roman glowered at me. "Do you have a problem with that? I don't like to see defenseless creatures suffer."

"You could at least give him a chance to recover."

"He does me no good if he can't show."

"So what, you discard something just because it isn't perfect?" Yeah, I was a little touchy on that point.

"I paid for perfection."

And now he seemed in a mighty hurry to get rid of what no longer suited him. But then why should he treat his horses any better than the revolving door of women who went through his life? "There are rescue shelters who'll be happy to take him and rehabilitate him."

Roman sneered. "This from the girl who almost got him killed by a dirt bike."

"That wasn't my fault."

As if I wasn't worthy of any more of his attention, he turned back to the vet. "I want a report by six."

Patrick Dunhill, who mostly liked to watch his empire from the turret of his mansion, stormed in. Hind tumbled out of his office to meet him.

"Things like this don't happen in my barn," Mr. Dunhill said to Roman. "I've already arranged for extra security."

"It's a little late for that, isn't it?"

Mr. Dunhill's face shook and purpled with his contained rage, emphasizing the whiteness of his hair. "Mr. Hind will ensure that your horse gets all the care he needs."

"What are you doing to find who did this?"

"The police—"

"I pay good money to keep my horses here. I expect them to be safe."

"I agree completely with you," Mr. Dunhill said. "We're doing everything we can to remedy the situation."

"I want the stable closed. It's Saturday. Everybody and their brother will be showing up to ride. I want the scene contained until we find who did this."

"The police have released the scene." When Mr. Dunhill weighed the irritation factor of thirty angry clients against the possibility of losing one—or two, if Ross followed his brother's lead—the majority won. "*All* my boarders pay good money to have access to their horses during business hours. Saturday is our busiest day. As I said, I've added extra patrols, but we *will* remain open."

No sooner had Mr. Dunhill spoken than a group of well-heeled riders and their entourage walked in, unaware of the charged atmosphere.

"I'll be taking my horses elsewhere."

"You're welcome to it." Mr. Dunhill's reputation ensured that the stalls weren't going to stay empty for long, scandal notwithstanding. He turned on his heel and left, Hind following behind.

Ross walked up as the vet left, face dark with concern as he stroked Bandit's neck. "How's he doing?"

"How does it look like he's doing?" Roman said, raking a hand through his hair. "He's dying. This is your fault. This was supposed to be Firewall."

"We'll get him the best care we can."

"It's too late. His show days are over."

Roman hiked away and, I swear, the air got lighter. The man definitely had a chip the size of Everest on his shoulder.

"What is it between the two of you?" I asked, slowly urging Bandit back toward his stall.

Ross blew out a breath. "Long story."

One he obviously didn't plan to share with a mere groom.

Forehead furrowed with concern, he nodded toward Bandit as I released him in his stall. "Make sure Bandit's as comfortable as he can be."

Like I'd do anything else. I rolled my eyes and caught a slight twitch of his lips. Ross reached out and skimmed a knuckle along the bruise on my cheek and I wanted to rub against his touch like a cat. "Nasty bruise."

"You should see the other guy." Of course, if I'd done my job right, the other guy would be in custody.

"You are something else," he said as he entered Firewall's stall.

The place soon buzzed like a salon on prom day. I needed to collect a tissue sample from Bandit's leg for analysis. Sure, the vet would do the same, but he wouldn't likely share the results with me. But Hind kept me busy with extra chores, punishing me no doubt for everything that had happened.

I climbed to the loft and got down the hay bales for the next feed. As I held the first bale, ready to call "Heads up!" and let it fly, I spotted a thin man hanging just below the chute. He was trying too hard to look as if he belonged. With so many owners and their friends and family swarming around, the task was easier for him to accomplish. But something about the way he looked around like a fox choosing a fat hen put me on alert.

The black ball cap lowered all the way down to his eyes, shading all of his face, and the black windbreaker he wore on this warm spring day certainly didn't help his case. Nor did the bulge beneath the material. What was he hiding there?

The clop of shod horse hooves on concrete had him straightening. From my position, I couldn't see who was coming our way. He reached into his jacket, paused, as if waiting for his victim to get closer. As he started to draw out his hand, a flash of silver glinted in the sunlight streaming in from the open door. Crap. The guy had a gun. Acting on instinct rather than plan, I let go of the bale. Bull's-eye!

The guy was knocked on his can. His ballcap flew off, revealing a shock of red hair. Horse hooves scrambled backward and Leah Siegel's voice filtered through the ceiling cracks. "Whoa, Waldo. Whoa, it's okay, baby."

The gunman shoved away the bale and bounced to his feet. He looked up at me, then at his target and reached inside his jacket once more.

I launched another bale and jumped down after it, landing on a mass of hay and human, barely feeling the jolt of socket against residual limb, and held him sprawled on the concrete floor with all my weight.

Small, close-set eyes threw menacing daggers at me. He bared his teeth, flicked the lighter he held in his left hand and jabbed the flame at my face. Rolling partway off him, I cat-kicked, aiming at his wrist, and heard a satisfying snap as the metal ankle of my prosthesis connected with bone.

"Get off me!" Howling, he jerked up his legs, trying to roll me. But he couldn't gain momentum before I rammed my reinforced right knee into his groin. This prosthesis was coming in handy after all.

He squealed like a wounded pig, drawing Hind out from the feed room. A small crowd of curious onlookers trickled in behind the barn manager.

"What the hell are you doing now?" Hind barked at me.

"He's got a gun," I said, holding down my writhing prey.

"I don't have a gun," the man screamed in a high, thin voice. "I'm not armed. Look for yourself."

Hind jerked his head at me. I removed my leg from the man's groin, but held my grip on his arms.

Hind proceeded to open the jacket. Out popped a pack of cigarettes. I glanced at the fallen lighter. Silver.

Oops.

"Fire hazard," I choked out. "He could've set the whole place on fire."

Hind pushed aside the other half of the jacket and

uncovered a camera and a set of credentials from the *New York Reporter*. His face turned marble-hard, and his glare had the poor photographer shaking.

"Call the cops," Hind said to Dawn. Smiling with devilish delight, she nodded and trotted away.

"No, I can explain." Beads of sweat collected in the dip of the man's upper lip. He worked his jaw and scrambled backward like a crab. The hay bales and the wall cornered him. "I got a tip. All I wanted was one picture. I've got to feed my kids, you know."

Hind continued his glacial stare.

The man licked his lips. "You know a good celeb shot is worth extra. Come on. Give me a break here. They say Leah Siegel got a nose job. That it got botched. That's why she's been out of the circuit since December. All I wanted was one shot. Swear to God."

Who would have started that rumor?

"Sit on him till the cops get here," Hind said to me. "I want him charged with trespassing and assault."

"Hey, she's the one who assaulted *me*."

Hind smiled a truly terrifying smile. "That's not the way I saw it." He reached down for the pack of cigarettes and the lighter. The man flinched, drawing his arms up as if to protect himself from a punch. Hind lit up, puffed a few times, making the end glow red, then squashed the cigarette under the toe of his workboot. He then returned the pack and the lighter to the photographer's pocket.

"I saw you lunge at my groom after she asked you to put out your cigarette," Hind said. "How about you, Ally? That how you saw it?"

I was flabbergasted. Hind taking *my* side. No, I corrected myself, he was protecting his clients. They would expect no less for the amount of money they paid for board. "That's the way I saw it, too."

When I looked up, I met Ross's laser gaze burning me with the heat of suspicion.

Chapter 7

Ross had disappeared before the skulking-photographer episode was settled with the police. I'd seen more of the boys in blue in the past few days than I had in my previous twenty-five years, which I found slightly disturbing. I needed to ease Ross's suspicion, but I couldn't very well do that if he wasn't around. In the meantime, I had to keep up the appearance of being nothing more than an unlucky groom.

As I walked Azur for a turnout at pasture, the phone in my pocket vibrated. I glanced at the caller ID. Alan. It was about time.

I let the mare loose, then rested my foot on a lower

fence rung while I wolfed down another energy bar. God, those things were awful.

"I'm going to need a second dead drop picked up," I said, patting the pocket that held the empty aspirin bottle I'd cleaned for the purpose of housing the sample. I gave Alan the short version of last night and this morning's incidents.

"I'll send the tissue sample to a specialist," he said.

"How long before you get results?"

"At least a day or two."

I couldn't keep disappointment from seeping into my voice. "Bandit may not have that long."

"This isn't *CSI,* darling. In real life it takes longer than an hour to get results."

"Right." Patience, I reminded myself, was an essential tool of any investigation. It just wasn't my strongest quality. "Let me know as soon as you hear back."

"Something interesting popped up on the backgrounds."

Keeping my eyes roving for anyone approaching, I said, "Oh?"

"There's a juvenile record on Erin Mays."

"Erin?" I supposed time in juvie could explain her obsession with keeping her job in a place she considered home. "Aren't juvenile records sealed?"

"Darling," Alan all but purred. "I have my ways."

About which I was probably better off not knowing too much. "What kind of record?"

"Theft."

"Felony?"

"No, but multiple offenses," he said and paused dramatically. "Breaking and entering."

Interesting. "In Connecticut?

"Florida."

Where the Horse Ripper started his spree.

"Oh, and her name isn't Erin Mays. It's Erica Sholes. I'll keep digging."

"Anything on Mandy's whereabouts?" I asked.

"She's working at a farm in upstate New York. Courtesy of Renee after she found out about the firing."

So much for the easy solution. The fired groom had been a dead end from the beginning.

Paper rustled on Alan's desk. "I have an update for you. The mystery liquid we picked up last night is henna."

"Henna? Isn't henna red?"

"According to Kristi, the Indians used henna to keep their hair dark and shiny. This black formula is a natural extract that won't harm the horse's sensitive skin like a commercial hair dye would. That's probably why he has to reapply it often."

I pursed my lips. "Why would Ross be dyeing Magnus?"

"The only reason I can think of is theft."

"But why would Ross need to steal a horse? He can buy any horse he wants." He already owned a multimillion-dollar Olympic hopeful.

"*That* is a good question."

Was Ross involved in something illegal? I don't know why that thought saddened me so much. There had to be a way to find out who the horse really belonged to.

A gust of wind swept through the trees lining the paddock, shaking the leaves. I shivered in spite of the late-afternoon heat.

"Alexa?"

An idea formed. "Pull up the VetTech Web site."

"Done."

"They have an animal ID service, don't they?"

"Ident-a-Horse and Ident-a-Pet. Um, interesting, they also have a service for humans. Can you imagine?"

I couldn't.

But people who owned horses as expensive as the ones housed at the Ashcroft Equestrian Center would want a foolproof way to identify their animals in case of theft. A freeze brand or a lip tattoo could fade or be altered, but the grain of rice-size microchip implant was permanent and didn't leave a scar—another plus for a show horse. I know I'd protected both my horses with implanted chips from a rival company.

"Get whoever's picking up the tissue sample to drop off one of VetTech's scanners." If Magnus's neck was tagged with a chip, the scanner would display the number, then Alan could check the database and tell me who the chip was registered to. Maybe then I could figure out what Ross was hiding.

A cloud of dust lifted from the road, and a horse trailer turned into the equestrian center's drive.

"Were you able to get anything of the big project Hardel Industries is working on?" I asked as I tracked the trailer's progress.

"I'm working on it. Tough place to crack. They have more security layers than the Pentagon."

I recognized the logo on the side of the trailer, and my heart sank to my boots. "I have to go. The vet's here for Bandit."

The weight of failure dragged my feet as I made my way back to the stables. I'd come here to protect horses, and Bandit was about to be put down.

What if my earlier thought was right? What if the Horse Ripper's killings were a distraction for the real target? The biker was hired to spook Bandit, not Firewall. And Bandit was the intruder's victim. Switching the placards to make the victim look like the wrong target was easy enough. "Alan? Can you get me a copy of the vet records on Bandit? And find out if he's insured."

"I'll see what I can swing."

The answer was here somewhere. In plain sight. All I had to do was find the right place to look.

By the time I reached the stable, the vet was already back at his trailer, readying to load.

I rushed inside, sick at the ease with which Roman could condemn a horse simply for not being perfect.

"Where have you been?" Roman asked, eyebrows bunched in annoyance. "Get Bandit ready to travel."

"You're putting him down?" A stone of sadness lodged in my chest.

"That's really none of your business."

Desperation to save a perfectly good horse from slaughter had me clutching at straws. "I'll buy him from you."

"You can't afford him."

I had an eight-digit trust fund. I could afford the whole darn stable. But not without blowing my cover. "I'll pay him off in installments."

"I'll chip in," Erin said, peeking out from Cause Célèbre's stall.

Roman made a sound of impatience and disgust. "He's in pain. He's never going to get better."

"Grant Montney rehabilitates horses. He could—"

"He's my horse," Roman warned in a rough tone. "I want him out of his misery."

"What's going on?" Hind asked. He had a knack of catching me at my worst.

"She's not obeying orders," Roman snarled.

"I was simply offering an alternative."

"You're not paid to think," Hind said. "Get your ass in gear or take it elsewhere."

My hands tightened into fists. I couldn't blow my cover. Not with the Horse Ripper still on the loose and the show coming up. So, clenching my teeth, I sucked it up and stalked to Bandit's stall.

With tears pinching my eyes, I slipped his halter over his head. The poor thing's face was wrinkled with pain. "I'm sorry."

"It's probably for the best," a gentle voice said behind me. I turned to see the vet, whose face drooped with despair. "The damage is so extensive that I'm not sure I could repair it. And since we don't know the causative agent, we have no way of stopping the spread."

I stared at Bandit's back legs. The wounds had sprawled from cannon to hock to gaskin and were reaching toward the thigh. "The tests didn't tell you what was injected?"

He shook his head. "He's in terrible pain."

Unable to speak, I nodded as my trembling fingers stroked Bandit's muzzle.

And just like that, the vet spirited Bandit away, leaving his stall empty—a stark reminder of my failure.

Anger drove me to push myself harder. I dropped off the tissue sample for Alan's courier. Too late for Bandit, but maybe it would give me a clue to follow. I drew up a mental list of suspects, then tried narrowing them down. Frustration ate at me like acid and all I had to show for my effort was a pounding headache.

Tonight, though, I hoped one of the pieces would fall into place.

* * *

I waited until everyone was asleep before slipping from my room into the brisk wind that howled around the house. I had to be more careful than usual because Mr. Dunhill had increased the security patrols. I retrieved the cell-phone-size scanner from the dead drop just as the first spatter of rain started speckling my hair, then dashed to the stable. The arena lights were on. Was Ross here for another late-night ride? I decided there was no point creeping around. If a guard showed up, I'd just tell him I was here to help Ross.

I strode to the arena, then crossed my arms over the top of the gate and watched the heart-stopping lines of man and horse moving as one.

Ross spotted me as he brought Magnus down to a trot. If he was surprised, he didn't show it. He cooled Magnus down and, when I saw him coming my way, I held the gate open for them.

"Barn Goddess?" he asked as he clipped a crosstie to one side of Magnus's halter in a wash stall while I did the other side.

When I frowned, he pointed at the faded slogan on the red T-shirt I'd slipped on after my shower. "Yeah, that's me. Goddess of the Manure Pile."

He laughed and his gaze did a slow crawl from my breasts to my face. "I can think of a nicer way to put it. But goddess fits."

My cheeks flamed broiler-hot.

"So what are you doing here so late?" he asked.

"Pretty obvious, I'd say. Bandit was put down today. It just about killed me to load him on the vet's trailer, even though my head, if not my heart, knows it was the right thing to do. I'm with your horses most of the day. I've grown attached to them. I came to make sure they were okay. Besides, sleep is over-rated." I unbuckled the girth. "Does Hind know you're here this late?"

"He knows."

"I guess that's why the guard didn't sound the alarm. Do this often?"

Half his mouth curled up, but he didn't answer.

I placed the saddle on a holder. "So, I saw you jump Magnus. He can jump."

"A little bit."

"That's like saying that Firewall is just a pony. You both looked great." And incredibly sexy. I concentrated on unrolling the hose. "Is there a reason you train him in the middle of the night?"

"Scheduling problems." Ross removed Magnus's splint boots.

I wasn't buying that one bit. "You could've told me, and I'd have helped you out." As I was beginning to suspect Mandy had. Or maybe his reputation as a cad was overstated. Maybe he didn't fight it because it suited his stealthy purpose.

"So, level with me," I said as I turned on the hose. "Why are you hiding Magnus? Too much stuff is happening around here. If you expect me to protect him, I think I have a right to know what's going on."

The laser blue of his gaze seemed to see right through my disguise, and I forced myself to concentrate on bathing Magnus.

"I've received some threats," he finally admitted.

"For all your horses or just Magnus?"

"All of them." Ross hesitated. I sensed there was a but he wasn't sharing.

"From the Horse Ripper?"

"I'm not sure."

"Written? Verbal? Electronic?"

He rubbed his eyes. "What difference does it make?"

I shrugged and turned off the hose. "It could give us a clue."

"Us?"

He had a bad habit of driving me to exasperation. And, I realized, I'd almost blown my cover. "Yes, us. Me, you, everybody who works here. The police. Have you noticed the cops have been here almost on a daily basis?"

"I've noticed. Mandy gets fired. I get a new groom. Bad things start to happen." He pegged me with a look that set my heart galloping with the fear of discovery. "I'm not liking that coincidence."

Winning his trust wasn't going to happen anytime soon. I shrugged and met the challenge in his eye with my best poker face. "Call it the curse of bad luck. I've got more bruises on me than an apple in a

cider press. Besides it's pretty much the pot calling
the kettle black. You seem to attract your own share
of negative attention."

"Why did you jump the photographer?"

"He didn't look right."

"How?"

I shrugged. "I don't know. Sneaky. I thought he
had a gun and he was aiming for Waldo. I thought he
might be the Ripper. Better safe than sorry, right?"

He grunted. "If I didn't know better, I'd think you
were an undercover cop—or something."

My throat went desert dry. *Careful, Alexa. Play it
cool. He doesn't know anything. He's just fishing.*
"Yeah, I'm actually an FBI agent. You know like
Sandra Bullock in that movie where she goes undercover at a beauty pageant. My bank account sure
could use a second paycheck. What do you suppose
an FBI agent makes?" I finished scraping excess water off Harrison. "It's gotta be better than what Dunhill pays. Do you think FBI agents need a degree?
Cuz now that you've brought it up, a career change
might not be such a bad thing."

Ross opened his mouth as if to say something,
then shook his head. "Smart-ass."

After Ross left—and this time I made sure he was
truly gone before I sneaked back into the stables—I
backtracked to Magnus's stall and pointed the scanner at the place on his neck where the ID chip should
lie. I was rewarded with a beep that said my hunch

had proved correct. There was an electronic marker buried in the muscle of Magnus's neck.

Finally I would get some answers about Ross.

I dialed Alan and read off the number on the scanner's display. He would call me back in a few minutes. I sat in the back corner of Magnus's stall, and a weight settled on my heart at the thought of Bandit's empty stall.

I'd joked with Ross about being an undercover agent, but Bandit's empty stall was no joke. Nor were the deaths of the Horse Ripper's other victims.

If the Horse Ripper struck again, could I stop him? I swiped at unwanted tears that tasted of failure. Going down that defeatist road wasn't going to help the horses or me.

I had years of experience as a horsewoman, if not as a groom, and the Gotham Rose Club had put me through intensive training. I had as good a chance as anyone else to catch the bastard.

I didn't just have something to prove to Renee and the Governess. I had something to prove to myself.

Magnus lowered his head and blew hot breath against my hair as if in reassurance. I stroked the prickly soft velvet of his muzzle and sniffed his hay-sweetened breath.

"I wish you could talk and tell me your story."

The phone vibrated in my lap. Just as I flipped it on to answer, the stable door rolled on its steel track and footsteps echoed down the concrete aisle.

"Hang on," I whispered to Alan. "Someone's coming." I held my breath as the guard peered into Magnus's stall. Five agonizing minutes later, the guard went out the door at the opposite end of the building.

"Go ahead," I told Alan.

"The chip's registered to Hardel Industries."

I frowned. "That doesn't make sense. If Magnus is his horse, why dye him?"

"His name isn't Magnus. The horse that belongs to that number is a gray one called Indigo Flash."

Indigo Flash? "The name doesn't sound familiar."

"Apparently, three years ago someone slipped him cocaine before his Grand Prix class and he went ballistic. He crashed through a six-foot jump, flipped and landed on top of his rider."

I shuddered and blinked away the flashback to my own accident. "How badly was he hurt?"

"The press clippings say the horse was put down due to nerve damage to his back—he couldn't walk."

That fit with what Ross had told me about Magnus recovering from an injury. Somehow the thought he hadn't lied to me about that made me feel better. "Who was riding him?"

Alan's fingers set his computer keys clacking. "You won't believe it. Roman Hardel."

Electrified, I jumped to my feet. "Roman! Ross is hiding the horse from his own brother?"

"Apparently," Alan said. "And according to Kristi, black is the easiest color to dye a gray horse."

A whole new set of possibilities raced through my mind. Why was Ross hiding the horse from his own brother? "You'd think he'd have recognized the horse, anyway, if he'd owned him."

"Darling, how often do males notice things like new hairdos or outfits—unless they're gay?" Alan chuckled at his own joke.

Ross's intelligence went up a couple of points in my esteem. Hide in plain sight. But why was he hiding the horse in the first place? Because he'd created the Horse Ripper to get back at his brother for the injury he'd caused Indigo Flash? Or did Ross suspect Roman was the Horse Ripper? The thought that Roman had hurt Bandit on purpose made me sick. Had he sacrificed him to make himself appear above suspicion? Or had he tried to implicate Ross by switching the name placards?

I simply didn't know. And I had to find the answers fast—before another horse was hurt.

I had one more day to put the clues together before the situation got more complicated. Tomorrow we left for New York and the showgrounds. The place would teem with strangers, giving the Horse Ripper even more ease to hide right under my nose.

The mood at the stables was somber the next morning. Bandit's empty stall was a grim reminder for everyone that tragedy had visited what they'd thought was a safe haven. The Horse Ripper wasn't supposed to get to a horse on Patrick Dunhill's turf.

And everyone had pretty much decided something this vile had to be the work of the Ripper.

Show preparations went into high gear. Riders squeezed in last training sessions. The farrier checked feet and shoes. And Hind handed me a long to-do list, then kept harping at me that I was doing things wrong. The clipping was uneven. The bandages weren't rolled right. The equipment wasn't stowed correctly in the travel trunks. Belting him wasn't an option if I wanted to keep my job, so I finally just tuned him out and did the best I could.

As low groom on the totem pole, I drew the short straw and would ride with Jesse, the maintenance assistant, who would drive the farm's red truck and white six-horse trailer. Dawn and Erin left after lunch to set up stalls, tack rooms and feed stalls and make sure everything was ready for the horses when the trailer arrived.

Cause Célèbre balked as we approached the trailer. I tried to sweet-talk him, but he wasn't listening. His heartbeat rippled against his side as if he were afraid of the trailer. "No bogeymen in there. Just sweet hay. Come on. Up you go."

But the horse pulled back on the lead, shivering and staring wide-eyed at the trailer.

"I don't think I've ever seen a groom as incompetent as you are," Roman groused. He snatched Cause Célèbre from me and attempted to load him himself. When the gelding wouldn't cooperate with direct manhandling, Roman got a whip and whacked it against the horse's rump.

Personally, I thought that was a mistake. If someone took a whip at me, especially if I was scared, I'd kick. Which is exactly what Cause Célèbre did. Then he scampered back down the ramp. Sweat soaked his shoulder. His nostrils flared as wide as if he'd just run a mile.

Roman swore. "There's no point in getting him more riled up. We'll stay here tonight so he can calm down and try again in the morning."

His killer glare put the blame squarely on my shoulder.

He handed the horse to Katelyn, who slanted me a snotty little smile of satisfaction.

"Unload Trademark," Roman bellowed at me. "I don't want to do two trips. He'll go with Claudine's horse tomorrow."

Hind wasn't happy and turned on me. "You've really messed up this time. If I didn't need every hand I have, you'd be out the door. Load up Sweet Charity and Canyon Moon instead. We need a full load on both trips."

By the time we were ready to go, the sun set in a bruise of purplish-black clouds that promised rain. Jesse made a detour to the maintenance shed to pick up the bag of sandwiches and a thermos of coffee he'd brought with him for the ride. "To keep me awake," he said with a grin. "Strong and black."

He and Ross conferred over the route they'd take. I wasn't driving; I didn't care.

"I'll be right behind you," Ross said and trotted to his Jaguar.

Knowing what Magnus had survived, I didn't take Ross's concern as a complaint against my skills.

Jesse went through what looked like a flight check by a pilot. He turned on the radio. "What music you like?"

"You're driving. Your choice." That had been my father's rule when I complained about the opera he liked to sing along to.

"Country okay?"

I nodded. I didn't mind. My own stablehand kept a radio tuned to a country station while he worked.

He lifted the Thermos. "Coffee?"

"No, thanks. Will it bother you if I sleep?" I needed the rest.

He showed me a full display of yellowing teeth and laughed. "Not if my singing doesn't keep you awake."

"I'm so tired, I could sleep through a tornado."

Jesse shoved a hand out the window and gave Ross a thumbs-up, then crammed the truck in gear. With a rumble of the heavy-duty engine and a lurch, the truck rolled forward and down the driveway. The purring roar of Ross's Jaguar trailed behind us. As soon as we passed the red brick pillars of the entrance, fat drops of rain spattered against the windshield. Jesse turned on the wipers, and they kept time with Joe Nichol's fast-tempoed "What's a Guy Gotta Do."

Less than ten minutes later we were on I-84 and on our way to Pier 94 in New York City. Home. I sighed and sank deeper into the seat.

In the glaze of rain, the lights along the highway dazzled like precious jewels—white diamonds, red rubies, amber topaz. Wet blacktop shone, strands of licorice whips streaking beneath the wheels of the traffic ahead of us. Even this late, loaded trucks of all kinds clogged the road and provided a steady hum.

"Pour me another cup of coffee," Jesse said, "then take your siesta. I wake you when we get there."

I didn't need any convincing. I poured Jesse's coffee, then, head resting against the rain-chilled window, I thought of the city, of home. It seemed much longer than five days since Renee had handed me this assignment. I thought of my apartment and its fluffy white pillows and quilted feather bed, of the spa tub with its relaxing jets, sighed with yearning for my familiar little luxuries and promptly fell asleep.

The jarring tattoo of tires rolling on the drunk bumps alongside the road startled me out of my dose. High in the cabin of the truck, I looked down on the road. Where were we? A curve was coming up and it looked as if we weren't going to take it.

"Jesse?" I asked, jolting out of my cramped position.

No answer.

His head drooped against his chest, bumping up and down with each jar of the road. His loose hands looped over the steering wheel at six o'clock.

Oh, God, he'd fallen asleep.

Chapter 8

I yelled at the unconscious maintenance assistant. "Jesse! Jesse! Wake up!"

No reaction. Landscape blurred outside the truck.

Magnus. The horses. I couldn't let them get hurt.

I shook Jesse harder and yelled louder, straining against my seat belt to turn the steering wheel into the curve. "Jesse! Wake up!"

Jesse's lax body fell against me. The movement pressed his sleep-heavy foot farther down on the accelerator, thrusting the truck even faster. His slack hand jostled the steering wheel. We drifted left into the next lane and into traffic. Horns honked. I couldn't reach his leg to yank his foot off the accelerator and slow the rig.

A semi raced by, horn blaring. His draft pounded the truck and drenched the windshield with a blinding slew of water. The hapless driver of the Saturn behind the semi cranked the wheel too fast, too hard, skidding the car into a spin. Its bumper clipped the truck's running board and the grind of tearing metal echoed in the truck's cabin. Pieces of fiberglass from the Saturn clanked against the window. The impact wobbled the horse trailer and rocked the truck from side to side.

A whinny of fear trumpeted from the trailer and lodged my heart in my throat. Petrified horses scrambled for balance. *Hang on.*

While steering, I gave one last desperate effort to wake Jesse to no avail. Once I was going straight again, I let go of the steering wheel and fumbled with the seat belt release. With a click, it gave way, allowing me to slide closer to Jesse.

I grabbed the wheel with one hand and fought the building wobble. I slid as close to Jesse as I could and hiked my legs over the gearshift. He wasn't a big man, but he was dead weight and I sat in an awkward position. I grabbed the back of his shirt and hauled him across my lap. Lifting all that hay and manure had built some muscle, but I managed only an inch or two of progress before his shirt ripped.

I cursed.

"Do you want to die, Jesse?" I pounded a fist in the middle of his back. He didn't even flinch. "Wake up! Now!"

Panic swarmed through me, shallowing my breath and slicking my palms. I couldn't possibly drive this rig. I'd never driven anything this big. My right foot wouldn't feel the pedals.

I gritted my teeth.

All I had to do was slow down and get to the side of the road, I reminded myself, concentrating on the fast-moving blacktop. "Get on the side of the road. Stop. Get help."

I repeated my plan like a mantra as I grabbed the waistband of Jesse's jeans. With a heaving groan, I hoisted him far enough to get fully into the driver's seat. I felt for the brake pedal with my left foot. Even though I was desperate for this wild ride to end, I pumped lightly, knowing that slamming the brakes on this wet pavement could cause the trailer to flip. I sobbed a gasp of relief when the truck finally started to slow.

Just as I started to relax, air brakes, loud and shrill, shrieked behind the rig. The deep blast of a fast-moving semi's horn sounded a warning that blared inside me. The big truck loomed much too close, its headlights glaring in the side mirrors. God, no! He was going to hit the trailer.

For the first time since I'd joined the Gotham Rose Club, I realized that being an agent wasn't about excitement or assignments or even proving myself. It was about making life-and-death decisions under pressure and accepting responsibility for the outcome.

I wasn't willing to sacrifice these horses. Not after what had happened to Bandit.

With a white-knuckled grip, I manhandled the truck onto the shoulder, praying the trailer wouldn't sway into the semi's path. The weight of the trailer pushed the truck forward. I strained against what felt like G-force, but what seemed a lifetime later, the rig stalled and came to a stop just before an exit ramp.

The semi boomed by us, buffeting the truck, barely missing us.

I'd done it! I was still there. Shaky, but still there. And Jesse and the horses were safe.

Ross, dripping wet, eyes snapping with fury, wrenched open the driver's door. He looked down at the man's boots still in my lap. "What the hell's going on? You're driving like a maniac. There are valuable horses back there."

I looked into his scowl unable to let go of the steering wheel. I couldn't stop the violent shaking of my arms and legs. "Jesse—passed out," was all I could muster.

The draft from passing traffic slapped us with cold wind and splashed us with rain.

"What happened?" Ross stretched across me and felt for Jesse's pulse. "He's breathing."

"I'm not sure." My voice was thin and shaky. "I was sleeping, then he hit the drunk bumps and I couldn't wake him."

Ross didn't look as if he believed me as he pulled

out his phone and dialed 911, relaying the situation in an authoritative voice that strangely calmed me.

I gulped in air and spotted the Thermos on the floor of the truck's cab.

Ross switched off his phone. His glare had an accusatory note to it and his tone was hard. "What's the last thing you remember before falling asleep?"

"This *isn't* my fault. I poured Jesse a cup of coffee like he wanted to keep him awake. And the next thing I know, we're riding the drunk bumps." A knot of horror mushroomed inside me. I reached for the Thermos, screwed open the top and sniffed at the contents. "Maybe someone drugged his coffee, but I don't smell anything." I thrust the Thermos out at Ross. "Do you?"

He didn't accept my offer and scrutinized me as if I were somehow responsible for knocking out Jesse. "I don't like this."

So much for us getting anywhere in the trust department. I squirmed even though I didn't have anything to feel guilty about.

Then I got pissed. "Do I need to remind you that *I* almost died? That *I'm* the one who kept your horses in one piece?"

He mumbled something that might have been an apology, but the tone sure wasn't sincere.

"Why would anyone want to hurt Jesse?" I asked, still shaky.

He glanced at the trailer. "Magnus is in there."

"So are Firewall and Waldo," I reminded him. "Come to think of it, your brother conveniently managed to get his horse and Claudine's off the trailer. There's a coincidence for you."

He grunted but didn't stand up for his brother. There was definitely something odd going on in that family.

"Does Roman have a reason to hurt you or your horses?" I asked.

He shook his head but didn't elaborate.

"If there's something between you and Roman and the horses, I need to know. It almost cost me my life."

He raked a hand through his hair, then looked me up and down. "You scared the hell out of me. I was keeping an eye on the truck, then all of the sudden it started weaving. I couldn't do anything to stop it."

"Trust me, I wasn't having a picnic. I've never driven a truck before." I swallowed hard. "Will Jesse be okay?"

"I don't know." Then Ross almost smothered me against his chest and kissed the top of my head. Slowly heat returned to my numb limbs. His body was solid against mine, the drum of his heart prompting mine to slow down. The depth of my contentment in his arms was almost as frightening as the wild ride.

"About your brother?" I asked.

"I'll deal with him." The note of finality said there would be no more discussions on that subject.

A kick against the side of the trailer reminded me of my duty. Doing something would ease the web of frustration tightening through me. "The horses."

"Stay. I'll go." He turned the heat up high. Not that it did any good with the engine off. Then he wrapped his leather jacket around my shoulders and headed to the trailer to check on the horses. His residual heat and his saddle-soap scent hugged me, even as Jesse's stillness beside me gave me the creeps. I tried to reassure him. "You'll be fine, Jesse. The paramedics'll be here any minute now."

The wail of sirens approached and the red and white lights of the ambulance gave the night a macabre look. I jumped out of the cab and directed the two paramedics to Jesse.

"What happened?" the first paramedic asked while the bald one jumped in the cab to check vital signs.

"I don't know. I was sleeping and when I woke up, he was passed out at the wheel."

"Does he have any medical conditions?"

"I have no idea." I watched them check over Jesse. "What's wrong with him?"

"He's coming to." The bald paramedic sprang out and went to get a gurney.

"We'll take him in and have him checked out," the other said.

"Where are you taking him?" Ross asked.

The paramedic rattled off the hospital's address.

"We can't let him go to the hospital on his own," I said, watching the ambulance pull away. Waking up to unfamiliar faces was scary, grown man or not.

"We can't very well park the rig and leave six horses standing," Ross said.

"You're right."

"We'll call after we get the horses settled," he said to mollify me, and I nodded.

A state trooper arrived. I was getting really good at giving statements. By now the cops probably had a warning beside the name Ally Cross. *This girl is a magnet for trouble.*

After the trooper left, Ross slid into the driver's seat and I climbed in on the passenger's side.

"What about your Jag?" I asked, glancing at the hunter-green sports car parked rather crookedly behind the trailer.

He started the truck and checked the mirrors for oncoming traffic. "I'll have it picked up."

"Aren't you afraid someone's going to steal it or chop it up for parts?" We weren't exactly in the finer part of the state.

"It's just a car," he said, and merged into the traffic.

An hour later, we pulled into the showgrounds on Pier 94. The huge building consisted of a stable area with 231 stalls, all decked out as homes away from home. At regular intervals canvas drapes in owners' colors were attached to stall walls to make private tack rooms, feed rooms and dressing rooms. Some went as far as to lug real wood furniture, hang art and pretty up with faux turf and real potted plants.

On the other side of the office, fifty-eight vendors

had set up shop to provide everything from tack repair to fancy chapeaux for the parties. A food court along the back wall of the merchant area served a menu that varied daily.

Neither Dawn nor Erin was anywhere in sight when we finally arrived, but the horses' stalls were all ready. As if he'd done this a time or two, Ross helped me bed down the horses.

After they were settled with water and hay, Ross checked on Jesse. The doctor was keeping him overnight for observation. Jesse's wife and daughter were already with him, so he wasn't alone, which relieved me. Hospitals were scary places.

The blood test results would take a few days. But I already had a hunch something of the chemical persuasion would show up laced among the red and white blood cells.

Ross glanced at his watch. "It's late and it's been a hell of a day. Why don't we grab a bite to eat?"

Although several private security guards were hired to watch over the six horses we'd brought in today and the six coming tomorrow as well as our equipment and supplies, I planned on spending the night in the dressing room where a cot was set up for catching naps during the five long days of the show. I was feeling too raw from my multiple failures to allow the Horse Ripper to get anywhere near the horses. My job was to keep Waldo, Firewall and Magnus safe.

"I'm really tired," I said and an uncharacteristic ripple of disappointment wafted through me. I needed extrastrength pain reliever and, at the very least, to massage the abused skin of my residual limb. A shower and change of clothes could wait until the other grooms showed up in the morning. "I'm just going to call it a day. I'll see you in the morning."

"Some other time?"

I was so tired that I thought I detected a hint of regret in Ross's voice. Or maybe he just felt bad for being a jerk and accusing me of wanting to kill his horses. "Sure. What time do you want Firewall saddled?"

"I'll have to check the practice schedule." He was staring at me again. Worse, I could feel that weird something inside me giving again.

I found a quiet corner and called in my report and arranged for someone to pick up the coffee sample I'd snagged before the trooper bagged the Thermos. The maintenance assistant was strong and healthy. His sudden keeling over couldn't be natural. Alan's results would come in faster than the doctor's or the police lab's.

As I bedded down in the cot in the dressing room, surrounded by the quiet sounds of horses resting, part of me wished I'd taken Ross up on his dinner invitation. Those electric-blue eyes. The sensual fullness of his mouth. A tiny string of desire plucked deep inside. Before I could ponder the error of this train of thought, exhaustion barreled over me and knocked me out.

* * *

The horse show was basically an excuse to party and, late on the next afternoon, the place teemed with both exhibitors and spectators.

The crème de la crème of New York's social scene would show up. Each sponsoring charity would ask them to whip out their checkbooks and make a generous donation in exchange for a memorable night out.

Tonight, opening night of the five-day show, Horses of Hope, my charity, would host a wine-and-cheese party on a private yacht on Chelsea Pier after the special therapeutic program exhibition and the Dressage Royal Cup.

My not being there would raise some eyebrows—notably my mother's—but that couldn't be helped. Renee would step up for me as hostess. I had to maintain my cover.

The big event, of course, was on Sunday. A ball following the show-jumping Grand Prix would close the festivities.

The hospitallike security bracelet at my wrist allowed me access to the standing-room area of the show arena. I'd convinced Erin to stay and babysit the horses while I grabbed dinner and peeked in on the event I'd planned. I stabbed at a salmon Caesar salad with a plastic fork while keeping an eye out for anything out of the ordinary.

Handlers and their special-needs charges roamed

around the staging area, readying for their demonstration for Vice President Kelley's wife, Anne.

Rosemary, my assistant, ushered Anne and Renee to the table of honor center stage. I was relieved to see Rosemary had solved the dilemma of who was going to sit with the guest of honor. Renee flanked Anne on one side, and Mayor Siegel, elegant in Armani, and Leah, overpowered by a brown-and-cream DVF wrap dress, sat on the other.

Anne's explosive laughter rebounded across the arena. The yellow Oscar de la Renta suit she wore reflected her sunny personality. She'd already won the hearts of many Americans with her warm, yet nononsense attitude.

When President Mason's term was over in three more years, she would go far to help her husband secure the White House. As a fellow dressage enthusiast, she had my vote. Um, there was a thought—maybe *she* should make a run for the presidency.

Other tables in the Diamond Circle preferred-seating area, reserved for the chic and deep-pocketed, filled up fast. Upper-crust regulars and celebrities shone in all their fineries, making the tables look like a photo shoot for *Vogue*.

Anne turned to Renee, her booming voice reaching me. "Where's Alexa tonight? I wanted to talk to her about a special project I'm working on that would mesh well with her foundation's mission."

I couldn't hear Renee's reply, but I was sure she

made a suitable excuse for my failure to attend. I doubted anyone in the VIP seats would recognize me in my groom disguise, but just in case, I lowered the brim of the gimme cap I'd borrowed from the dressing room.

A few minutes later Renee opened the event for me. "Ladies and gentlemen, welcome to a very special evening of horsemanship. I'd like you to help me welcome Mrs. Anne Kelley. She's here tonight not as the vice president's wife, but as an avid horsewoman.

"Mrs. Kelley has been a staunch supporter of therapeutic riding programs, and we're hoping that her presence here tonight will entice you to dig deep into your wallets to help Horses of Hope and their life-affirming programs.

The crowd roared with applause, and Anne graciously accepted their acknowledgment. "It's my great pleasure to recognize the Horses of Hope Foundation and the inroads it has achieved in advancing therapeutic riding programs all over the country. Horses of Hope has provided grants to start programs and to keep those programs insured as well as supplied with trained and certified instructors."

With a sweeping look that reverberated with strength, she continued, "As a child, I was labeled learning disabled, an academic underachiever, and if they'd had the term at the time, ADD would probably have been added to the already loaded slate.

"I hated myself. I thought I was stupid and a loser.

Changing schools didn't help. My failures just followed me and bloomed anew."

I'd never known that about Anne Kelley. She always seemed so sure of herself, so full of energy and ambition.

"Then I met Cinderella," Anne continued, her eyes crinkling with humor. "No, not the princess of fairy tales, but a fat, white Connemara pony with large brown eyes and a penchant for peppermint candy. She became my best friend and showed me a part of myself I never knew existed. She gave me back control in a world that was nothing but chaos. Despair gave way to determination.

"I went on to achieve more than I ever expected." Anne's self-mocking smile beamed at the audience. "And now no one can stop me."

The audience laughed along with her.

"We have with us a few of those special riders whose lives have been enriched by participation in these hippotherapy programs sponsored by Horses of Hope.

"Let's give a big round of applause for the great strides forward these riders have taken."

Anne clapped. A roar went up.

A little thrill went through me as I watched the first rider nudge the pony beneath him. A small boy with cerebral palsy, who looked around twelve, rode through a line of cones, an assistant on each side. Pride shone in his face as he fought the spasms of his body to guide the horse instead of movement just happening.

A fourteen-year-old boy with Down's Syndrome showed how he could steer through a small obstacle course, praising his pony for the triumphs that were his.

The doctors had told the seventeen-year-old teenager with a brain injury that she'd never walk again. Now here she was flying over a jump.

Once classified as an incorrigible juvenile delinquent, a fifteen-year-old girl now danced with her horse in a breathtaking dressage demonstration.

And a ten-year-old boy showed that arms were optional when it came to controlling a horse.

Tears fuzzed the picture in front of me, his fearless courage shaming me for my refusal to let anyone see the less-than-perfect side of me.

"Hey." A teenage girl with a boyish cut came to stand beside me.

"Hey." I recognized her. Haley, Renee's daughter. Had she recognized me? I ducked my head and hunched up my shoulders, watching her out of my peripheral vision.

When had she cut her waist-long, golden-blond hair? Her gray eyes showed both a touch of defiance and a sea of unhappiness. Her makeup had gotten edgier since I'd last seen her—thick emerald eye shadow, ringed with black liner and eyelashes that curled to unnatural lengths. Her black jeans were ripped at the knees. Her black beaded micro top more suited to a lady of the night than the daughter of a prominent society lady.

Fifteen trying to pass for twenty-five.

I clucked silently. Her father's being in jail put her under a lot of stress. One of the psychological riding therapy programs would probably do Haley some good. But Preston was being released on Saturday, so maybe she'd be okay.

"Some show, huh?" Haley said and sucked on the straw of her megasize soda with pouty lips, leaving behind a blood-red mark. "I know someone like that."

"Like what?"

"Handicapped. She's missing a leg. You'd never know it, though."

"Um," I said, the buzz of wariness needling through me.

"You'd think that she'd do like Anne Kelley and let everyone know so she could rake in the money for her foundation."

"What, play the pity card?"

"Why not? It's for a good cause."

How did Haley even know about my leg? Other than the Governess, Renee, the agency support staff and the agents who'd trained with me, no one was supposed to know. "Is that so?"

She squinted at me. "You're Ross Hardel's groom, aren't you?"

I nodded.

"Do you know where he is?" Her voice got breathless.

"I have no idea."

"Do you think he'd mind if I went to visit Firewall?" A bit of hope widened her eyes, making her look her age for a moment.

"You can't get into the stable area without a pass."

Haley lifted her skinny arm and brandished a security bracelet like mine. "I've been bugging my mom to get me a horse, but she says I haven't 'demonstrated enough diligence to shoulder responsibility.'" She snorted as she made quote marks in the air with two fingers of her free hand. "As if! She just doesn't want me to have any fun."

Wow. That sounded familiar. Had Renee taken mother-daughter relationship lessons from my mother?

Speak of the devil, there went Jacquelyn Cheltingham all perfect and polished in a Prada brocade evening jacket that exactly matched the champagne of her hair. My father, as usual, was notable for his absence.

"Well, since you have a pass," I said, and I needed to get back to the horses, "I guess I can take you to see Firewall."

I pushed myself off the boards, hoping I'd been fast enough to avoid detection from my mother's inappropriate-behavior-sensing radar. And she would definitely consider my Levi's and faded T-shirt inappropriate for this venue.

The security scanner beeped us through into the stable area. I pitched my empty fast-food plate and the rest of my milkshake into the trash. Haley took one last draw of her soda and did the same. Our block of fifteen stalls was at the far end of the stall area.

As we walked down the right-hand aisle, Haley shoved both hands in her back pockets, thrusting her B-cup chest and lifting up the tip of her shirt's triangle hem high enough to show off her bellybutton diamond. "So what's he like?"

"Who?"

"Ross Hardel."

I shrugged. "I don't know. Like all the owners. Arrogant and clueless."

"I think he's hot."

I made some sort of noise, but Haley was lost in her own little world and didn't notice.

"I've seen him ride," she said. "I wouldn't mind having those hands all over me."

My eyebrows hiked up. "Isn't he a little old for you?"

She jerked a shoulder carelessly. "I like older men. They're, like, experienced."

As if she would know. I angled a glance her way. Or did she? At fifteen—preaccident—Nat and I had certainly obsessed over boys and sex, but it was all theory and supposition. Haley might just be in enough pain to take talk over the line into action.

"I hear he's great in bed," Haley said.

"How would a kid hear something like that?"

"I'm not a kid." Her bottom lip plumped into a pout. "Besides, I hear things."

We were almost at the Ashcroft Center's stalls when someone yelled, "Heads up!"

I glanced over my shoulder in time to see a runaway propane-powered forklift coming right at us.

Chapter 9

The driverless forklift hurtled backward right at us.

The mad beeping revved my pulse. Haley screamed. I lunged at her, shoving her out of the way and into the storage area. The machine whooshed by and slammed its back end into the side of the building where it bounced and came back at us, forks ready to slice us in half.

Still screaming, Haley tried to find purchase on the concrete floor, but her slick-soled shoes kept slipping.

Vaguely aware of the din of chaos shooting up, I grabbed Haley by the arms, "Come on."

I rolled us between two fifty-gallon drums. The

forklift's metal tusks speared into the top of the barrels and crunched into the wall above us, raining chunks of concrete onto our heads. Fear widened Haley's eyes until white gleamed all around the iris-wide pupils and made her throat work spasmodically.

The engine roared like an enraged boar. The wheels spun against the metal drums, burning rubber. The creak of metal slowly buckling boomed in my ears. I scrunched us both farther down.

Amid the shouts and hysteria, someone finally reached for the ignition switch and killed the engine.

"Someone call 911," I heard a male voice shout.

"Swear to God, I have no idea how this happened," someone else said.

"You okay down there?" Concerned brown eyes peered at us in our gloomy cave beneath the forks and body of the forklift.

"We're fine," I managed, holding a hyperventilating Haley. "It's okay, Haley. We're okay. Shh. They'll get us out of here in no time. Just breathe, Haley. We're okay."

"I want my mom."

"We'll get her." Having placed her daughter in danger would certainly do nothing to raise my esteem in Renee's eyes.

As my heartbeat slowed, I pictured the original path of the forklift. Was it meant to kill me or crush Firewall's stall? I didn't like either possibility.

The pounding of boot-shod feet approached and

a stripe on a navy pant leg flashed by. "Security. What's the trouble here?"

"Runaway forklift," a man said, his gravelly voice shaky. "I don't know how it got away. I swear to God, I turned it off. I was gone for a second. No more than five. Swear to God."

"There are two girls caught between the barrels," someone said.

"Back up, folks. Show's over," the security guard ordered. "Let's back it out so we can get the girls out," he added to the forklift operator

"The machine's stuck in the wall," the forklift operator pointed out. "Turning on the engine could crush 'em."

As the forklift driver and the guard argued about the best way to free us, Haley stirred against me. She tipped her head up, eyes wide. "You're her, aren't you? You're Alexa Cheltingham. I can feel your leg against mine and it's not flesh!"

Oh, great. After all I'd gone through to transform my looks and maintain my cover, it was the damn metal of the workout leg that gave me away.

"Clear the way!" both guards shouted.

The forklift operator climbed into the contraption and fired the engine.

"Haley," I said above the din. "You can't tell anyone. Do you understand?"

"Why not?"

The forklift shuddered and she winced.

"Because," I said, biting my bottom lip with my top teeth. How much could I say without putting my assignment or the Gotham Rose agency in jeopardy? "No one can know. Especially your mother. It's important."

"Why?"

My mother used to say that there wasn't much difference between a two-year-old and a teenager. I was beginning to see what she meant. *Okay, so get Haley where she lives—the land of high drama.* "It could mean the difference between life and death."

"Really?" Excitement rippled in her voice.

"Really." Which was actually a little too close to the truth for comfort.

The wheels strained against the metal barrels, crushing them a little more. Haley squealed and turtled closer to me. I held on to her tightly. With a final groan the tusks broke free, taking the barrels with them. The whole machine convulsed, then shot backward. I coughed as concrete dust showered down on us. The engine died midrumble.

I scanned the crowd. Was the Horse Ripper watching? I didn't see Ross. Or Roman. But Claudine was talking with Juliane's mother.

"Hang on, girls." Several pairs of hands reached to pull us up.

Haley's legs wobbled as she blew out air and she ran both hands through her short hair. "I could really use a cigarette."

"Those things'll kill you," I said, dusting concrete

off my jeans. I couldn't help thinking back to the cigarette case in my purse with the half-smoked reminder of the day my world shattered. "I'll walk you back to your mother."

"But I didn't get to see Firewall."

"He's not going to be in the mood for visitors after a fright like that."

"But—"

"Look, I have to go check on the horses. I don't have time to babysit."

She sulked. "I don't need babysitting."

"Once your mother hears about this accident, she's going to be upset."

"Like she cares," Haley scoffed.

"She does."

"Not that I see."

There was no point arguing with a teenager. They saw what they wanted to see. "Fine, help me check the horses then."

Claudine and Juliane's mother stopped us.

"Are you all right?" Juliane's mother asked.

Claudine smirked. "Well, you sure have a way of attracting trouble. I'm glad you're not my groom."

Both Dawn and Erin were busy calming the horses. They all seemed fine. Haley petted Firewall's neck. "Yeah, I'd really like to get a horse of my own."

"I'll talk to your mother."

"Would you?" Her gray eyes shone with hope.

I shrugged. Having something to love might jar her out of her self-defeating rebellion. "Why not?"

Fifteen minutes later I led Haley back to find her mother.

"Haley?" I said at the entrance, spotting Renee in the VIP section. "You'll keep my secret?"

She glanced at her mother, weighing no doubt the pros and cons of juicy gossip against being one up on Renee. Finally she beamed me a pleased smile. "Okay."

As I watched Haley hurry to her mother, safe and sound, the phone in my pocket vibrated.

I needed fresh air, so I headed outside to the small park beside the pier and whipped out my phone.

"You're working late," I said to Alan as I settled into one of the benches overlooking the Hudson River and scanned my surroundings. Every muscle was tensed for flight and eyes seemed to hide in the folds of darkness.

"A thankless job, but someone has to do it," Alan said with uncharacteristic melancholy. "I have some news."

"Good, I hope."

"Depends. The lab found traces of Ambien in the coffee sample you sent."

Sleeping pills. "No wonder Jesse was dead to the world."

What was worth the cost of innocent lives?

I licked my dry lips and heightened my visual patrol of the area. The Horse Ripper wasn't going to win. I wasn't going to let him. "Anything on the tissue sample from Bandit's leg?"

"My guy's having a hard time isolating the caustic substance. He's sending it on to a pal of his at Cornell."

Cornell University did a lot of the drug testing for horses. "How long before we know something? Security is as tight as it can be, but with so many people going in and out of the showgrounds at all hours, there's plenty of opportunity for someone to slip in and gain access to the horses. Sunday is only four days away."

"Do you want answers or guesses?" Alan asked, a bit of petulance peppering his voice.

I sighed. "Answers are always best."

"Then be patient." The staccato gunfire of computer keys clicked in my ear. "I also have something on Dawn Waller."

"What about her?" My gaze narrowed as I took in the lanky guy whose foot jiggled nervously against the lamppost. Why did he keep looking my way?

"She deposited a large sum of money in her savings account yesterday," Alan said.

"How large?"

"Ten thousand dollars," he said. "I know, pocket change for you, darling, but for someone like her, a small fortune."

The intruder who'd hurt Bandit was definitely male. As was the biker who'd said a man had paid him—of course, he could be lying. Bribe money? For drugging Jesse?

"Do you have the source of the money?"

"Cash."

Good old anonymous cash left no electronic footprints.

"I'll see if I can get her to talk about it," I said, but didn't hold my breath. How did you slip that kind of windfall into a conversation in a natural way?

"I also got a peek at Bandit's vet records?"

"What did you find?"

"The vet noted X-rays taken a few months ago after Bandit turned up lame after a show. From what I can make of the doctor's jargon, Bandit didn't have the legs left to go much further in his career."

"So Roman could very well have wanted to have him killed accidentally so he could reap the insurance money." Instead of paying someone to take him off his hands.

"Except that all the Hardel horse are registered to Hardel Industries, not the individual sons. If there was any insurance money to get, the company would get it, not the brothers."

"Is the company in financial difficulty?"

"Not according to the quarterly report they just put out."

"Where's the motive, then?" I growled. "If not money, why would Roman want his horse dead?"

"I don't know, darling, but I don't like how the situation is developing. Be careful."

"No need to worry about that." I pocketed my

phone and surveyed the darkness beyond the yellow pools cast by the lampposts, my senses tuned for any threat.

I wasn't going to take any chances.

Word-of-mouth about the forklift incident had reached Roman. At Trademark's stall, he tried to loom over me but couldn't quite manage the feat because of my height. He was dressed to the nines in a black Dolce & Gabbana suit. No doubt on his way to the party I was supposed to be hosting.

"You've already cost me one horse," Roman spewed with a venom almost as caustic as the one used on Bandit's legs. "I'd like to get to show the one I have left."

I gritted my teeth. *The client is always right*, Hind had said. *Especially when he's wrong.* "Trademark was never in any danger."

He snorted indignantly. "He could have gotten crushed!"

"He was on the wrong side of the aisle." I refrained from mentioning that *I* was the one who'd almost ended up a pancake or that I now ached from head to toe and had bruises in places I never knew you could get bruises.

"All this stress isn't going to help him show his best on Sunday."

"Instead of tearing her to pieces, you should be asking her if she's all right." Ross's voice behind me sent a trickle like warm maple syrup down my spine. "She could have died protecting the horses."

Roman's sharp gaze skidded from me to Ross and bristled. "What was the damn forklift doing any-where near the stalls in the first place?"

"How should she know?" Ross argued, iceberg-calm to Roman's storm-tossed sea. Ross was still dressed in stable gear, I noticed. "She didn't drive it there."

The bead of spittle at the corner of Roman's mouth gave him a rabid look. "She should have an-ticipated the danger and taken care of it. She's paid to pay attention to danger."

The worst part was that he was right. I *was* sup-posed to anticipate and protect.

"She isn't paid enough to give her life to protect your horse or mine," Ross said.

Watching them toe-to-toe was eerie—like watch-ing a reflection argue with itself in the mirror. Blue eyes meeting blue eyes in a contest of wills. As the brothers butted heads, I had a feeling that it wasn't me or the horses or the forklift they were arguing about, but something much more personal. They were tak-ing sibling rivalry to whole new heights. Which nat-urally made me wonder how far they would take it.

Roman broke first. He speared me with a look close to hatred. "If anything happens to my horse, I'm holding you personally responsible."

Long, stiff steps carried him away before I could say anything.

"How is it that the person with the least power is saddled with the heaviest responsibility?" I asked rhetorically.

"Don't let him get to you."

"Easy for you to say," I scoffed. "It's not your job on the line."

"I think you're doing a great job."

"Yeah, sure. That's why you're here, too, isn't it? You heard about the forklift. Trouble. Ally. Coincidence. And I know how you feel about coincidence."

I turned to go. I so did not need any more attitude right now. He palmed my shoulders and turned me around. The laser of his gaze had a way of going straight through me and buzzing as if I'd been touched by raw electricity. "I meant what I said. Your life is too high a price to pay to protect a horse."

I was touched. Sort of. "Gee, thanks," I scoffed, brushing off my internal rattling at his nearness, at the comforting feel of his hands on my bruised body.

"I do care. More than you realize."

For a moment the way he looked at me, the blue of his eyes so hot, I thought he was going to kiss me, and worse, I wanted him to.

His hands fell from my shoulders. "Did you see who was driving?"

Maybe I made him uneasy, too, and that made me feel better.

"A ghost."

He slanted me a questioning look.

I pointed out the spot where I'd first noticed the machine and tracked its process down the aisle and into the storage area close to the equestrian center's stalls. "No one was driving. Looks like someone turned it on and aimed it at Firewall's stall. It got knocked off track, which is how it ended up coming right at me."

"Looks like I owe you—again," he said.

I shook my head. "That's my job. I'd do anything to keep the horses safe."

"I'm beginning to see that." He swept an arm toward the aisleway behind him. "Come on. Walk with me."

I glanced at Firewall contentedly chewing on hay. "I don't want to leave the horses alone."

"I appreciate that, but we need to talk. I won't keep you long, and the guards will keep a close eye on the horses."

I snorted. "Tell your brother that."

"Roman has issues."

"No kidding."

"It has nothing to do with the horses."

Oh, no? Then how come you're hiding his horse from him? Naturally, I couldn't ask *that* question.

Ross splayed a wide palm on the small of my back, sinking heated warmth into sore muscles. I almost sighed as he led me to the dressing room, which was set up for dinner. Two take-out boxes, along with two glasses that I could swear were Waterford crystal, sat on the small table covered with a silk scarf.

"Sit. I figured you wouldn't mind dinner. I haven't seen you eat much in the past few days and I know you're not sleeping."

The food smelled wonderful, but I couldn't help thinking that Ross had an ulterior motive up his sleeve.

"Shouldn't you be getting ready to go to the Horses of Hope wine-and-cheese party?" As hometown competitors both Ross and Roman's names were on the invitation list.

"I give plenty of money to charity." He pulled back the chair for me and I sat gingerly, feeling every muscle in my body stiffen from the bruising. I hadn't ached this horribly since the first week of agent training with Jimmy.

"Besides," Ross continued. "I've never cared for Alexa Cheltingham. I knew her when she was still in braces and she was an uptight little snob."

Me? An uptight snob? He was the one who was a twerp, always calling me Metal Mouth and Brillo Hair, then flirting with pretty Kati Coates whose petite figure was perfect and whose hair was long, blond and straight. "I hear her foundation does good work."

"There are plenty of programs as deserving of my charity contributions."

Watch it, Alexa. Riling yourself up will only blow your cover. "I suppose you're right."

He raised one eyebrow as he uncorked the wine

bottle. "And if she lies about her leg, it has to make you wonder what else she's lying about."

Tension strung me up from foot to neck. Did he know? "What do you mean?"

"She lost a leg in an accident and she went back to riding. But instead of using her triumph to inspire those she's supposed to help, she hides her handicap as if it's something she should be ashamed of."

Everything in me wanted to jump up and stalk away. I so did not need this crap. But I was supposed to be a groom and have no idea who Alexa Chelting-ham was. "Maybe she has her reasons."

"She's your typical two-faced Park Avenue prin-cess." He shook his head in disgust. "I can't imag-ine having to spend an evening with someone as fake as that."

"You'd rather spend it with someone who smells of sweat and horse?"

"Definitely." He eyed me again with that piercing blue gaze, and chuckled. "Can you imagine someone like Alexa Cheltingham scooping up manure and slopping feed rations?"

Oh, God, he knew. Every nerve ending went into overload. How could he possibly know? But if he didn't, why was he going on about Alexa? "You never know. She could surprise you."

"I doubt it. People like her don't stray far from their comfort zone. And hers is narrower than most."

Like he would know anything about me and how I spent my time.

"So, if you hate society girls so much," I said, "how come I'm always seeing your picture with a blond bombshell hanging on your arm?"

A tiny smile barely lifted the corners of his mouth. "You don't strike me as the kind of girl who'd read that sort of garbage."

I shrugged. "It's kind of like a car accident. You can't help looking. Especially when it's staring right at you when you check out of the grocery store."

He filled the wineglasses with a Chardonnay that was beyond Ally's ability to appreciate. "Most of the time it's Roman."

My eyes widened. "Really?"

"He likes to party. I like going to bed early."

Alone? I fought a rush of heat up my neck.

"Relatively," I said, thinking of his late-night rides with Magnus.

"Relatively," he agreed with a chuckle. "I'm expected to make certain appearances." He reached across the table, grazed a strand of my mousy hair, then wrapped a ringlet around the tip of his finger. A bolt of pleasure stabbed deep. "Personally, I've always preferred brunettes. Roman is the one into blondes."

I was *not* going to comment on that. Licking my lips, I tugged the strand out of his grasp and tucked it behind my ear. I opened the take-out box and the aroma of real food set off an embarrassing stomach growl. Time to get out of the gutter and back on track. "So tell me, what's between you and Roman?"

"I don't gossip." A window blind on greased lines couldn't have flapped closed faster than the way his eyes shuttered.

"It's not gossip if it's affecting my life."

His forehead wrinkled as if he thought there was something rattling loose in my brain. "How could our personal business affect you?"

"You've been standing up for me. He doesn't like you, so he takes it out on me."

"That's not very logical."

"Never underestimate the power of emotions. Especially the negative kind. If you guys are at each other's throat, I don't want to get caught in the middle."

He grunted and concentrated on his own meal. "I won't let anything happen to you."

"I don't need protection. I need to understand."

"It's family business, Ally. It has nothing to do with the horses. He's angry because I took an interest in the family business after college while he pursued another dream. His fell flat and mine is thriving."

"So it's jealousy?"

He jerked one shoulder. "It's a little more complicated than that. But, yes, basically it's jealousy."

"Is talking about the family business gossip, too?" I attacked the chicken breast with my worst table manners. He was already too suspicious and I needed to prove I didn't belong in his world. "What exactly does Hardel Industries do?"

"We deal in biotechnology."

I shook my fork at him. "Didn't I read somewhere that you'd bought another company recently? Vet-Tech? If you're into gizmos and stuff, why buy a veterinary supply house?" Keep it basic, I cautioned myself. Ally wouldn't understand the world of technology in which Alexa had grown up.

"To open the doors to a brave new world," he said as if he were kidding, which seemed odd.

"That sounds like science fiction."

"I suppose it is in a way. Sensoceuticals leverage the best of both biopharmacy and nanotechnology to create, well, miracles."

I picked up a whole green bean and folded it into my mouth, barely able to contain the shiver that lanced up my spine. "Miracles? Wow, that sounds impressive."

"The ideas have been around for a long time, but now we finally have the tools to try to bring them to life." His eyes glittered and I suddenly realized he was as passionate about his project as I was about my foundation.

I wasn't stupid. I could add. Secret project. Secret horse. Miraculous recovery. If it wasn't all somehow related I'd be surprised. "You're always at the equestrian center, though, so when do you go to work?"

He shrugged carelessly. "Maybe I shouldn't have said anything. For all I know you're a spy out to scoop my corporate secrets."

Heart tattooing against my chest way too fast, I lifted my wineglass at him and offered a mock salute. "Yeah, that's me. Ally Cross, undercover FBI agent *and* corporate spy. You'd think with all that extra cash flow I could get out of shoveling shit." I gulped down some wine, but it didn't do my dry throat a bit of good. "So, these miracles, how much are they worth?"

He leaned back in his chair and worked much too hard at appearing blasé. Oh, yeah, he had a lot more riding on this than a Grand Prix cup. "To us? Billions of dollars. To the receiver of said miracle? Priceless."

"Do you really think I'm after your secrets?"

"I hope not, because I like you."

"Me? Why?"

He leveled me with his sharp gaze again. "You're smart. You're easy to talk to. And you like horses."

I noticed he hadn't said beautiful and, yeah, that hurt.

"Can you imagine me at one of your fancy parties?" I snorted and almost tipped over the wineglass I was reaching for. Waterford crystal *so* didn't go with stained nails and scuffed knuckles. My manicurist would scold me for letting my hands get in such sad shape.

His gaze narrowed. "I think you can do anything you set your mind to. I think you're afraid, and that's why you're hiding. And I think you're underestimating both of us."

"Now what would I have to be afraid of?" I asked, latching on to the least frightening bit of his revelation.

"We tend to be afraid of things we want with too much passion. Because if we fail, it hurts too much."

The strain of hiding my anxiety was making me a little paranoid. He didn't know anything. He couldn't. "What are you afraid of losing?"

Leaning back, he crossed his long legs at the ankles. With a careless shrug, he tossed off an easy smile, but his downcast eyes spoke of deep pain. "Me, I'm careful not to care about anything too much."

"I don't believe you."

He frowned, insulted I wasn't taking him at his word. "And here I was baring my deepest secret to you."

"You were. Only someone passionate, someone who's had the experience of losing someone or something he cares about deeply could have said what you just said."

He gave a small nod as if ceding a point.

I narrowed my gaze at him, letting him know I had his number. "I think winning means more to you than you let on."

"Some would say winning is the only reason to pursue a goal."

"At all costs?"

He pondered the question, then he shook his head. "No. Some costs are too high. I don't want you spending the night here." Letting me know he knew just where I'd spent last night. How closely was he watching me? "We pay guards for that."

"I feel better if I'm near the horses."

"And I'd feel better knowing you were safe in your hotel room."

"There aren't any guards there," I pointed out.

"But there are locks and chains."

I could take care of myself, but there was no point arguing with him about it, especially if I wanted to keep my cover intact.

"About Roman—" I started.

"Everybody has secrets, Ally, and this one doesn't concern you."

The tone said there was no point continuing that line of questioning. I'd have to probe Dawn about Roman tomorrow. With the right question, she could go on and on.

"I'd better get to bed," I said. "Unlike some people, I don't get to sleep in tomorrow."

"Is that a challenge?" The electric blue of his eyes, the dip of his dimples on his beard-shadowed cheeks promised something sensual and wholly dangerous. The man was a menace. Worse, he knew it. I made myself recall each piece of evidence that colored him as a possible suspect.

"Knowing how important winning is to you, I don't stand a chance, so I'll cede you the victory."

"Too bad."

After I checked in with the hired guards to ensure they were both awake, Ross insisted on walking me to my hotel.

"Lock the door," he said once we got to my room. Our bodies were very close and my nerves started jumping. Back against the wall, I had nowhere to go.

He brushed his lips over mine. And though every sane brain cell shouted to hit the SOS button around my neck and pull away, I kissed him back and asked for more. His mouth was hard and hot and felt incredibly good. I was melting from the toes on up and didn't particularly want to stop. How humiliating that it took so little to make me want to surrender.

"Not a good idea," I whispered thickly. Not the way he felt about Alexa. Not with my cover in jeopardy of being blown to bits.

"I'll see you tomorrow." As he left, he wore a fiercely triumphant expression and I couldn't help feeling I'd just lost a round. But at what?

As I made my way to the bathroom in my ratty room, I wasn't sleepy at all. My body buzzed with a strange kind of energy, as if I could run a mile under four minutes and still have breath to spare.

One look in the bathroom mirror quickly extinguished any thoughts I might have entertained that Ross was interested in me personally—kiss notwithstanding. My eyes were ringed with fatigue. My tan had faded to an uneven white. The cat scratch and bruise on my cheeks added a street-punk edge. And all my hair needed was a For Rent sign and a rat could move in. Definitely nothing to inspire the dreams of a man like Ross.

How much did he know? And why was he toying with me?

Once in bed, I couldn't settle. Couldn't get Ross or his kiss out of my mind. Couldn't figure out what it was he wanted from me. I tossed and turned, worrying about the horses. It wasn't that I didn't trust the guards, but they didn't have as much riding on the horses' well-being as I did. Finally I gave up and got up, every stiff muscle protesting.

In the lobby, I spotted a coffee cart just opening. I bought a muffin to fill my stomach and a large to-go coffee to kick-start my brain and swallow down some aspirin. As I passed the lobby armchairs, a discarded newspaper caught my attention. The page was folded to Rubi Cho's "In the Know" column in the New York Reporter that sported a year-old photo of me in my Alexa Cheltingham incarnation.

Rubi wrote:

"What auburn-haired heiress failed to show up at her own charity's benefit? Her mother must be up in arms at having her daughter stand up the vice president's wife. Tsk, tsk. What a faux pas!

"And what dynamic duo spiced up the stall area at Pier 94 with a brawl last night? Spies say the showdown behind the scene mirrors some trouble brewing between the hunky brothers. Is there a woman involved? But of course! Stay tuned for more details."

I stuffed the newspaper in the garbage and hoped that no one would connect Alexa with Ally. Ross was already too close to the truth as it was. I had to find the Horse Ripper before Ross put the right pieces together and found the last thing he wanted—Alexa Cheltingham as his groom.

When I got to the stalls, I realized that the newspaper item was the least of my problems.

Something was terribly wrong with Firewall.

Chapter 10

Firewall staggered in his stall like a drunk as he tried to scratch his hide against the side of the stall. His appetite hadn't been as healthy as usual since we'd arrived at the showgrounds, but the vet had checked him over and found nothing wrong.

I placed an emergency call to Ross, the vet and Grant, as well as to Alan. Before everyone arrived, I collected samples of everything I could from feed to manure for Alan to have analyzed.

"What's going on?" Juliane's mother asked, worry crimping her forehead. "Did the Horse Ripper strike again?"

"No," I said, trying to contain the rumor before it spread panic. "I think it's a touch of colic."

Roman and Claudine, drawn by the small crowd at Firewall's stall, came to investigate. "What did you do this time?" Roman asked. "Have you managed to hurt another horse?"

"I told you to hire your own groom," Claudine added, lifting a penciled eyebrow. "This one attracts trouble like a dog attracts fleas."

"Just a touch of colic," I said, gritting my teeth to keep in my temper. "There's nothing to worry about."

But of course, that didn't stop the buzz of bad news. Uneasiness simmered and curdled into anxiety at the Horse Ripper having struck again. People made excuses to drop by Firewall's stall, and wings of dread fluttered across their faces at the sight of him. They demanded answers I didn't have.

The vet thought Firewall had developed a touch of laminitis, an inflammation of the sensitive laminae of the foot, and blamed it on Firewall's digestive problems since he'd arrived. He dosed him with anti-inflammatory medicine. But by nighttime, Firewall's condition had deteriorated rapidly. Lesions popped up on his body, and the whites of his eyes had taken on a yellowish cast. He could hardly walk.

White-faced, Ross called the vet again for a full workup. Part of me fretted at Ross's distress over Firewall's suffering. But I couldn't forget that he'd insisted I not sleep in the stable area last night. I should've listened to my instincts and come back sooner. Had Ross done this to his own horse? Or was Roman getting him back for Bandit?

My hands gripped the top of Firewall's stall, feeling helpless as I watched the big horse suffer. "I should've stayed with him last night instead of going back to the hotel," I said flatly, not caring if Ross heard the accusation in my voice. This couldn't go on. Whoever was hurting these innocent animals had to be stopped.

"It's not your fault," Ross kept insisting, but the deep lines bracketing his eyes betrayed his worry. "The guards didn't see anything. For all we know whoever got Bandit could have dosed Firewall with something."

Why wasn't he more upset? "But Firewall's the ticket to your dreams."

His eyes closed for a second and his shoulders sagged, but his voice remained firm. "My dreams are multifaceted."

"What do you mean by that?" Was he referring to whatever was going on between him and Roman? I wanted to strangle him until he talked.

Dawn's approach saved him from answering. She stood beside me at the stall, looking over Firewall's bumpy coat. "How's he doing?"

Alan had said Dawn had just had a big deposit added to her account. Could it have been payment to hurt Firewall? "He's not doing well at all."

"It always amazes me how little it takes to bring such powerful animals to their knees," she said, clucking.

Know that from experience, Dawn? "I can't stand seeing him like this. I wish there was something I could do."

"It's been happening too much lately," she agreed. "Erin and I are going to dinner. Want to come with?"

"No, I want to stay with Firewall."

Ross stroked Firewall's ear as I'd seen Persephone's massage therapist do. "Go."

My mouth fell open. "You don't trust me with him."

"I do, but there's no point in both of us sitting here watching him. He won't heal any faster. Go eat and you can take over for me later."

I chewed the inside of my cheek. The Grand Prix was only three days away. With one of the horses I was tasked to protect down, I'd already failed my assignment. If Dawn was the one who'd hurt Firewall, I needed to find out tonight before she could get to Waldo. "All right, then. Can I bring you back something?"

Ross shook his head, and I fought the urge to touch his arm as I left.

Dawn, Erin and I threaded through the crowd and headed outside to a hole-in-the-wall pub at the corner of Eleventh Avenue near Fifty-first Street. The Brown Bull looked like the type of place my mother had warned me to avoid. Two stories of soot-colored apartments plopped atop the restaurant. Faded brown paint and cream trim framed an opened door decorated with a neon shamrock and signs advertising beer. The sounds of a tin flute, guitar and fiddle plinking Irish folk music spilled onto the street.

The place was crammed with revelers and we had to fight our way to an empty table that squished us together too intimately and was too close to the band for real conversation.

I suggested we go elsewhere, but Dawn insisted the food was great here.

Sipping cosmopolitans with Porsche and Emma at Bemelman's was a whole different experience. Well, maybe not. Once Porsche had one too many, she could turn the place into chaos.

This place was a real meat market, exposing the raw side of testosterone. The six guys lounging at the bar, young and on the prowl—firemen by the looks of it—could easily set a calendar on fire if they took their shirts off. They contrasted with the dozen or so rough and rowdy construction workers who'd taken over several tables in the middle of the restaurant.

We shouted our order to the waitress, wearing a short green skirt and a cleavage-revealing white peasant blouse. As our food arrived, the band took a break and, once my ears stopped buzzing, I could actually hear the conversation around me.

"I heard Roman Hardel got on your case last night," Dawn said, reaching across her plate to mine and filching a fry. I pushed my plate toward her. If fries made her talk, she could have them.

"Yeah, I don't know what got into him," I said. "It's not like I wanted to get run over by a forklift."

"He's definitely wound a little too tight these days," Erin said, and knocked back the end of her beer. "I saw him ripping into Claudine during training this morning."

"What about?"

Erin shook her head. "I was too far away to hear, but it didn't look pretty." Her mouth crooked into a satisfied smile. "It was kind of nice seeing Claudine get some of her own medicine, though."

We all laughed.

I leaned forward. "So what's the deal between Roman and Ross? Why are they at each other's throats all the time?"

"Ah, brotherly love," Dawn mocked. "Roman thinks everything comes too easy for Ross. In a way, he's right. Roman has to work a lot harder to be half as good as Ross, but Roman doesn't see all the extra work Ross puts in when no one's looking at him."

"What do you mean?"

"Mandy used to go out to help Ross with Magnus late at night," Dawn said. "I'm surprised he hasn't asked you to take her place."

Me, too. Why was that? No matter how I looked at it, Ross wasn't being on the level with me.

Erin signaled the waitress for another round. "Roman doesn't even like riding."

"So why does he do it?"

"Daddy," Dawn and Erin said together, then giggled.

"A win by one of his sons is advertising exposure he can't buy," Erin said. "Or so I'm told. So Daddy's always pushing. He's a major sponsor at a lot of events and he wants return for his investment. And Daddy's going to be front and center come Sunday's event. Roman wants some of that Daddy praise."

"But why ride if he doesn't like it? It doesn't make sense. Why not earn Daddy's praise with something *he's* good at?"

Dawn stuffed the last of her corned beef sandwich in her mouth. "Because Roman's desperate to get Ross at his own game. To prove he's as good as Ross."

A chill of alarm raced down my back. Ross and Roman certainly brought sibling rivalry to new heights. But why wouldn't Roman want to stand out on his own merit? "Playing against your strengths seems stupid."

"No kidding." Dawn pushed her glasses up her nose and looked around to see if anyone could overhear. "They say Roman killed his mother. But it was all kept hush-hush."

What? Alan's report had mentioned the mother had killed herself twenty years ago. Was there any truth to Dawn's assertion? Maybe I was finally getting somewhere. "I'd heard it was a suicide."

"Yeah, that's what the family wanted everyone to believe."

"Wouldn't suicide cause as big a scandal as murder?"

"Not if she was murdered by her own nine-year-old son." Dawn's eyebrows rode up and her eyes bugged out. "They say Roman pushed her out their bedroom window because he was jealous of the attention she was giving Ross. Ross was sick with scarlet fever or some such disease."

"No!" No wonder Ross didn't want to talk about it.

"Yeah, and Roman tried to blame it on Ross," Dawn continued, delighted I was gobbling up her story with such avidity. "Ross was too weak to have gotten out of bed, let alone push his mother out the window."

Still, I was skeptical. "But how could a nine-year-old manage to overpower a full-grown woman?"

"I heard different," Erin said. "I heard it was Ross who did the pushing while he was hallucinating with a high fever."

I shook my head and rubbed at the chill raising goose bumps along my arm. What was killing a few horses after killing one's own mother? "That's some tale."

The waitress appeared with Erin's and Dawn's refills.

Dawn winked at me. "You should talk. You're making the gossip rounds with you jumping from the hayloft and squashing that reporter trying to take a picture of Leah Siegel."

"Moldy money, that girl," Erin said, pulling on her beer.

"Moldy money?" I asked.

"Old and a lot of it," Dawn said, honking. The beer was already hitting her hard. "I hear her father makes her beg for every cent he gives her. That's why she spends too much time at the stables. She can't stand being home."

Sad for Leah. She was a nice girl.

"She's not the only one whose father has a tight fist on the purse strings," Erin added. "Claudine is about to get kicked out of the center."

"Why?"

A round of laughter erupting from the group of firemen made me miss the beginning of Erin's answer.

"She's three months behind in paying her stable and training bills. Seems her daddy's gone over the bend and money's tight right now."

From the background information Alan had given me, I knew that Claudine's father was Claude Breitbach, the champion three-day eventer. Claudine had a younger sister who had been paralyzed as a teen in a riding accident and died of pulmonary complications a few years later. Her father never got over Stella's accident. He and his wife now lived on a modest farm in Virginia, and Claudine had taken over her parents' former New York City apartment.

Alan hadn't mentioned her financial difficulties—unless they hadn't quite caught up with her.

"Gone over the bend how?"

Erin hiccupped. "I heard Claudine say it was all Christopher Reeve's fault."

Talk about not taking responsibility for anything. Blaming her father's actions on a dead man took the cake. "The paralyzed actor?"

"Yeah, when he died, Claudine's father took it hard," Erin said. "Like it meant that they'd never find a way to cure paralysis because Chris was high profile and he wasn't around to push for more research. So Claudine's father donated a huge chunk of his fortune to the foundation Christopher Reeve started. Claudine is pissed because she thinks it's a lost cause."

"So she doesn't have anything of her own?"

"A modest trust fund," Erin said and threw a hand in the air. "Whatever the hell that is, but it's not enough to keep up with how she spends. If she spent less time at the salon and more in the saddle, she'd have half a chance at being a top rider."

"How close are she and Roman to marriage?"

Dawn and Erin both shrugged. "Probably closer in her mind than in reality," Erin said. "Not the way he cheats on her."

"Hey, you know what I also heard?" Dawn said. "That the reason Ross's horses are doing so well is that since Hardel Industries bought VetTech, he's

been able to feed his horses some sort of new research additive that doesn't show up on drug tests."

"I haven't noticed anything," I said, which really
didn't mean he wasn't slipping his horses something
when I wasn't around. And he could have acquired
each of the compounds used in the Horse Ripper's
attacks through VetTech. I really didn't like where
this was pointing. I'd seen the light of ambition burn
bright in Ross's eyes. What was the sense of hurting
Firewall when he was so close to Olympic gold and
all the glory that came with that?

A roar of laughter went up. My gaze drifted to the
group of firemen and the rookie clown who couldn't
seem to hold his beer. He'd pawed at the waitress
twice as she'd walked by with full trays. This time,
he hooked her by the waist and strapped her close,
slobbering her with unwanted kisses. She tried getting the attention of the bouncer at the door, but his
back was turned the wrong way. A grizzled construction worker who saw her plight puffed out his chest,
hiked up his jeans and went to the rescue.

"Mind your own friggin' business, old man," the
young firefighter slurred, shoving the construction
worker with one hand and tightening his hold on the
waitress's ass with the other. Chairs and stools
scraped back.

No way this was going to turn out well.

"Hey," I said to Erin and Dawn and pointed at the
brewing situation. I dumped bills on the table to

cover our tab. "We should get out of here before we get caught in that brawl."

As we wound our way between tables, someone grabbed Erin and tried to spin her into an embrace. I tapped him on the shoulder and smiled when he turned around. "My turn."

He dropped Erin, who fell to the ground, and reached for me. I pretended to go into his arms and kneed him where it counted. He doubled over, pushing into a construction worker and knocking over his beer.

The construction worker jumped up, tipping back his chair. As the firefighter and the construction worker exchanged fists, I grabbed Erin and headed toward the door.

We were almost free when sirens tore through the din and blue lights flashed right outside the door. I skidded to a stop.

"We can't get caught in this mess," I said. Sorting through everything at the station would take forever. "We've got horses to tend. With your fake IDs, you'd get busted." Mine would probably pass muster, but I sure didn't want to test Alan's proficiency.

Erin blanched. Dawn pushed her glasses up her nose, nodded and whirled around.

I propelled them back toward the rear exit. Someone grabbed my braid and yanked on it, pulling me off balance. I stumbled on a chair and crashed against a table, bruising my weak knee. Finally we reached the back exit. An alarm screeched as we plowed through the metal door.

"Come on. This way," I urged and headed toward the back of the parking lot. Skimming the barricade of the lot at a jog, we made it out onto a side street.

"That was close," Dawn said, the adrenaline rush brightening her face with exhilaration.

"Hang on." I stopped and hunched over, hands on knees, to catch my breath. Our shared near miss gave me an in to dig into Erin's juvenile record. "The last thing I needed was to get arrested."

"Me, too," Dawn agreed. "I think we should go over a couple of blocks before heading back toward the pier."

As we reached the other side of the road, I said, "I stole a lipstick when I was thirteen and the guard who caught me scared the snot out of me. No way I ever want to see the inside of a police station again."

Dawn's braying laughter echoed in the canyon made by the tall buildings. "I stole a pack of cigarettes on a dare."

"You got away with it?"

"I did, but I felt so bad, I never did it again. I couldn't smoke any of the damn things and ended up throwing the pack away."

"What about you, Erin?" I nudged her playfully with an elbow.

She shrugged. "After my mom died, I got caught stealing food a couple of times."

"Didn't you have anyone to take you in?"

She shook her head. "Social Services wanted to put me with a foster family, but I ran away."

"Why?" I asked at the next intersection. "You'd have had a home."

When the light turned green, she said, "I had plans."

"What kind of plans?"

"Mom said she had relatives up north."

"Did those plans work out?"

Erin kicked up the pace. "They will eventually."

They will eventually, echoed in my mind. She'd come from Florida where the Horse Ripper originated. Was there a connection?

But probing Erin's plans any further would have to wait until morning. Right before we reached Twelfth Avenue, she bent over on the side of the street and threw up.

Instead of going back to the showgrounds, Dawn and I, supporting Erin between us, took her back to the hotel and put her to bed.

I decided to grab a quick shower before heading back to the showgrounds to relieve Ross. My being there might not make a difference, but it would make me feel better.

But as I sat on the edge of the tub in my underwear to remove my leg, I found the release button had somehow snapped off and I couldn't release the prosthesis. The residual limb throbbed beneath the socket from the abuse of the past week and the long trek tonight. I desperately needed to take off the leg, escape my prison and let the skin breathe.

I poked and prodded and growled. I battered the ugly metal with my fist. I wanted to scream but bit my lips—the last thing I needed was to attract attention. My chest heaved and my throat worked as I tried to stop myself from crying.

I could barely see through my tears as I reached for my purse and pawed through the contents for the phone there. I was a professional. A trained agent. Professional agents didn't cry. This was a minor setback. I could handle it.

"I need to talk to Jimmy," I managed to say to Alan without revealing the depth of my misery. Alan's and Renee's numbers were the only direct ones I had. "It can't wait till morning when he comes in."

"I can take care of whatever you need."

"It's a leg problem," I said through clenched teeth, my face flaring from the sheer embarrassment of the situation. Some agent I was. I'd bet no one had ever called in needing help with such a stupid problem. Without further comment, Alan connected me with Jimmy at home.

"Hey, sweetheart, what's up?" Jimmy asked sleepily.

As much I as tried holding back the sobs, they broke from me in ugly, gasping rasps. "The release button fell off somehow and I can't get my leg off."

"Take a deep breath, sweetheart. You can fix this."

I sniffed and swiped at my cheeks with the back of my free hand. "How?"

"Do you have a screwdriver handy?"

"I have a pocket tool."

"Take the Phillips head, put it where the pin head was and the assembly'll release."

I riffled through my purse and located the triangular tool I carried for other emergencies. I did as Jimmy directed and sobbed with relief when the leg came off. "If you weren't married, I'd kiss you."

Amusement rolled through Jimmy's voice. "If I wasn't married, I'd let you."

Disaster averted, I took care of my residual limb, then headed back to the showgrounds. Jimmy's fix was temporary. I had to close this case before my leg fell apart.

On Friday morning, feeling the creepy crawl of eyes staring at the back of my neck, I surveyed the riders in the schooling ring and the spectators surrounding it while I waited for Leah to finish with Waldo. Forcing myself to appear relaxed, I leaned against the arena wall next to Dawn who was waiting for Double Vision.

"Wouldn't you love to be on the other side of the wall?" I asked, still hoping to get a lead on the ten-thousand-dollar payoff. "Nothing to do but ride in fine clothes and have someone else do the dirty work?"

She smirked. "Yeah, wouldn't that be the life!"

"Have you seen the dresses the VIP ladies wear to the shows?" I shook my head. "One of those designer outfits probably costs more than what I make in a year as a groom."

Dawn shrugged. "Well, I'm not planning on being a groom forever."

"Oh, yeah?"

Her eyes unfocused as if she were viewing an image somewhere far away. "I want a farm of my own. Nothing like the equestrian center. Just a place to raise a couple of horses, a couple of kids and give some lessons."

That dream seemed humble enough and reachable enough not to have to resort to killing horses. "You're saving up, then?"

"Todd'll be getting a settlement for his accident soon. Once he gets out of the rehab center, we'll start looking for a place. Todd likes Virginia."

"Who's Todd?" I'd seen a photograph of Dawn and a young man while I'd searched the grooms' rooms the day after I'd arrived, but she didn't know that.

A secret smile practically swallowed her lips. "My boyfriend."

"What kind of accident?"

"He was out training for one of his riders and part of the arena collapsed, crushing him."

"That's so awful. How is he doing?"

She shrugged. "As well as can be expected." But

I detected the note of lingering anger. Enough to take it out on the horses and their owners?

Still a settlement for an accident would go to Todd, not Dawn's bank account. Dawn raced away as her rider rode up to the gate.

I jumped as Juliane's mother, Karen, appeared at my side, her thin lips pursed as Juliane hopped over a fence. "Can't that trainer see the horse has no impulsion?" she mumbled. "Juliane! More leg!"

Juliane exaggerated a kick over the next fence, making Loophole refuse. "It's like she just doesn't want to win," her mother ground out between clenched teeth.

Halfway through the next set of instructions by Grant, Juliane slid off her horse in a torrent of tears. Karen Kallio, all tightly strung five feet of her, strode into the ring and blocked her daughter's path. She pointed toward the series of brightly painted jumps. "Get back on that horse this instant, young lady! We've sacrificed too much to get here."

Bawling, Juliane handed her mother Loophole's reins and bolted out the arena.

"Get back here this instant!" Karen yelled. A banshee couldn't have split the air more frightfully. Everyone in the vicinity stopped to watch the spectacle. When Juliane kept going, the mother yanked on Loophole's reins and practically dragged him out of the arena.

"Take care of him," she ordered me. "And make

sure he gets safely back to his stall." She glared at me with her coal-black eyes. "In one piece."

The fact that Loophole wasn't my charge didn't seem to faze her in the least. I followed the bickering mother and daughter. The clop of horse hooves provided a backbeat to the chorus of shouts.

"I gave up a good job so you could train. Your father switched his career so we could stay together as a family. How dare you be so ungrateful?"

"I never asked for anything."

"What is your problem?"

"I'm tired, Mom. I can't do this right now."

"Right now is the time to push. Later will be too late."

"But, Mom—"

"Don't 'but Mom' me. This win is important. Do you know who's going to be in the stands watching?"

"I don't give a shit."

Mrs. Kallio slapped Juliane across the cheek, leaving a red palm print. Juliane stared at her mother, body trembling as if she would break into pieces from the force of the blow and weight of her mother's expectations. Without a word, she turned on her heel and strode with military stiffness toward the exit.

"Juliane!" Her mother trotted after her. "Wait! Juliane, I'm sorry."

I handed Loophole to Dawn who shot me a questioning look.

"Same old, same old," I said.

I got back to the schooling ring for Waldo in time
to see Claudine collide with another horse. A squeal-
ing Cause Célèbre reared at the assault and dumped
Claudine against the ring wall. She crashed onto the
concrete walkway, screaming bloody murder.

"You're going to pay for this!" she yelled at the
frightened young girl into whom she'd collided, even
though her "I am alone in the universe" attitude had
caused the collision.

An ambulance was called to deal with her theatrics.

"My leg!" she screamed. "It's broken."

"You'll be all right, ma'am."

"It's broken," Claudine insisted. "Someone's going to pay."

Given what Erin had said about the state of Claudine's bank account, I wouldn't put a lawsuit past her.
How desperate was she for money?

The paramedics transported her to the hospital for
X-rays, but I suspected her pride was the only frac-
tured item. I was stuck handling Claudine's horse and
spotted Leah leaving the arena.

"I'll get Waldo for you as soon as I find Erin," I said.

"Don't worry about it. I've got him," she said and
led Waldo back to our stall area.

I'd just finished putting Cause Célèbre away when
my phone vibrated in my pocket.

"We need you to come in," Renee said in a
clipped tone.

Had I done something wrong? Nausea washed

through my gut as I remembered Ross's discussion of Alexa Cheltingham two nights ago. Was my cover blown? I focused on something less threatening. "Is this about Haley?"

"No, there's been a new development in the case. I'll send a car for you."

Chapter 11

With uncharacteristic silence, Olivia, Renee's assistant, led me into Renee's office. A fat bouquet of white tea roses spiced the air, masking my barn-ripe odor

"Renee will be right in," Olivia said as she slipped out the door and closed it.

My heart knocked around my chest, and a heavy feeling of doom shawled my shoulders. This couldn't be good. Had Ross or Haley blown my cover? I paced the room, the heels of my dirty barn boots echoing eerily against the floor.

"Alexa!" Renee breezed in, wearing a crisp Michael Kors suit and a three-strand necklace of pale-pink freshwater pearls. The quick squeeze of hand and air kiss she threw my way felt more like a hit-and-run. "Thank you for keeping an eye on Haley the other night. She told me Ross Hardel's groom allowed her to pet Firewall."

"A horse of her own might not be a bad idea," I said, thankful Haley had kept the forklift incident to herself. "It might turn her rebellion into something positive. There are programs—"

"I agree, but we'll discuss this later." She strode to her desk and punched the speakerphone. "Go ahead, Governess. We're both here."

Renee sat behind her desk and tented her hands over the white leather blotter.

"Alexa," the Governess's mechanically distorted voice sounded tinny over the speaker. "I want to thank you for the great job you've done."

"It's not over yet," I said, a bit puzzled. "I still haven't caught the Horse Ripper."

"The Horse Ripper is being apprehended as we speak."

My mouth fell open and I rushed to Renee's desk to stare at the speakerphone as if I could see the Governess through it. "Who? Where? When?"

"Alan's source at Cornell reported that the caustic substance that caused Bay Bridge Bandit's flesh to disintegrate was a form of brown recluse venom. We traced the spider venom to VetTech."

My heart pounded. Ross? Roman? "Who?"

The speakerphone squawked. "We located paperwork indicating that brown recluse venom was used for a short-lived experiment two years ago. The project was headed by Karen Kallio."

"Juliane's mother?"

"She has a degree in biochemistry and is highly motivated to see her daughter win. She was a member of the research staff at VetTech until the family moved to Ashcroft last August. The Kallios participated in the winter circuit in Florida. And all of the horses harmed were horses with the potential to cheat Juliane out of wins."

It all made sense. Perfect sense.

But it didn't add up with what I'd experienced at the equestrian center.

"Karen Kallio wasn't the person who hurt Bandit," I said with certainty. "I chased a man out of Bandit's stall."

"We found an empty vial of spider venom in Karen Kallio's home. She could have hired someone to inject the venom."

"Then why would she have the vial in her home? She doesn't strike me as stupid. If she'd done it, she'd have discarded the evidence. And why take the risk of someone betraying her? She knew how to inject the venom. She had access to the stables and would have attracted less attention at the stables than a perfect stranger. Anyone could have planted the vial in her home. This is a distraction tactic."

"We're not relying on one piece of evidence," the Governess said. "There is a trail that can't be ignored. The records show that Karen Kallio signed out a sample bottle of the neurological agent that brought down Blue Ribbon Belle a week before she resigned."

"You have the wrong person," I insisted.

Dead air hung in the room, making it hum with high-wire tension.

"We're pulling you out, Alexa," Renee said, gentling her voice as if that could cushion the blow of her lack of trust in my judgment. "We no longer require an agent in the field."

"Did I somehow blow my cover?" I asked, fisting my hands, thinking of Ross and how close he'd flirted with the truth.

"No, your cover is fine. Your presence at the showgrounds is simply no longer required."

"Why? The show isn't until Sunday. If I'm right and Karen is just a scapegoat, then Waldo is still at risk." And Magnus, and Ross's secret project. A billion-dollar payoff, he'd said. He'd received threats. But the Horse Ripper didn't know which horse to attack because Indigo Flash was undercover, so he'd had to have an excuse to kill repeatedly until he hit the right target.

"We've found the Horse Ripper," Renee insisted. Her mouth firmed and her eyes grew dark with temper. "The case is closed."

"No, listen, Karen isn't the Horse Ripper. She was

nowhere near the horses that got sick. She's too focused on Juliane—"

"And Juliane hasn't been living up to her high expectations." Renee's tone was like that of a teacher to a naughty kindergartener.

The speakerphone spit static before the Governess's voice boomed through. "Alan's contact says that Firewall's condition is due to ragwort poisoning, which also happens to be a research project at Vet-Tech. One started by Karen Kallio several years ago. She had access to the weed."

"No one had access to Firewall," I said between clenched teeth. "I fed him. I brushed him. I took care of his every need. The feed stall and horses are under twenty-four hour guard."

"Alexa—" Renee started, but I interrupted.

"Have you thought about how convenient it is that you've found the Horse Ripper just before the Grand Prix? Just before someone could take down a billion-dollar project?" This was a nightmare.

"Magnus is the real target," I continued. "Not Waldo. Not Firewall. Magnus, who is really Indigo Flash. Haven't you read my reports? After a bad fall, he couldn't walk. Now he's a Grand Prix hope. All in three years' time. Ross is dyeing him to protect him until he can prove the effectiveness of whatever it is his company did to heal him." And maybe Ross had tried to seduce me last night to buy my loyalty. But I wasn't going to share that.

"Alan's research into Hardel Industries doesn't support this claim."

"So you automatically assume that the information I've given you is wrong? The fact that Alan couldn't dig up anything corroborates the lengths to which Hardel Industries has gone to keep the project under wraps. Someone obviously wants to make it look as if VetTech is linked to the Horse Ripper. If the company's credibility is in question, then their big hush-hush project will have credibility problems. And that leaves room for someone to cash in on their success while they're battling their tainted image. Their stock would plunge. Their project would die." And with it, the hopes of thousands— human and animal.

"Alexa—"

"My cover's still intact. I still have time to find out who's doing this. Even if VetTech is involved, don't you want the truth?" My nerves were a buzzing hive ready to swarm. "*Please,* Governess, this is more complicated than it looks."

"Do you have concrete proof of any of this?" the Governess asked tersely.

"No, but—"

"Then I must side with the hard evidence we have in our possession."

"Renee," I implored, feeling my insides unravel like an old sweater.

Renee's face remained impassive as she laced her

fingers together. "I agree with the Governess, Alexa. The situation is contained."

"You aren't in the field. You haven't seen Indigo Flash. If Hardel Industries has managed to make a paralyzed horse walk again, think of all the people who would benefit from this technological breakthrough. Think of all the people who'd want to get their hands on that technology. Why even the Duke would—"

Renee's face fell with disappointment. "Alexa—"

"I'm sorry, but I can't quit now." I pushed away from the desk and stood straight, every fiber of my body vibrating with the certainty of what I had to do. "Indigo Flash is still in danger. I have to stay with him."

I'd already lost two horses. I wasn't going to lose this one. Not even if it cost me my acceptance as a full-fledged agent in the Gotham Rose Club. This was a life-and-death decision and I'd live with the consequences.

"You've been given a direct order, Alexa," the Governess said, leaving no room for argument. "We're pleased with what you were able to accomplish. You've proven you are an asset to the Gotham Rose Club. Why don't you take a few days off?"

"I'm going back to the showgrounds," I said obstinately and wheeled toward the door. A vignette of faces from my years of working with Horses of Hope flashed in front of my eyes. It was no longer just Magnus's life at stake, but the lives of thousands of injured people who would benefit from Hardel Industries' project.

Renee caught my arm. "This is not the time to let your impetuous nature get the better of you. Don't let your blinders destroy what you've managed to accomplish."

I wasn't being impetuous; I was being true to myself, to the mission of my foundation. And for once I didn't care what anyone else thought of me. I couldn't show weakness and back down from something so important. I had to protect Magnus

"How am I going to explain just leaving like that?"

"Grooms quit all the time."

"I don't. I'm going back to the showgrounds," I said stubbornly. "I'll stay with Magnus until the Grand Prix is over on Sunday."

I may have failed as an agent, but I wasn't going to fail as a person.

"This is for your own safety," the Governess warned, "There are circumstances we can't share with you at this time."

I was on my own. So what else was new?

I yanked on the silver locket, breaking the chain holding it around my neck. I opened my hand and dropped the electronic safekeeping device that connected me to the Gotham Rose Club. The locket clunked against the glass surface of Renee's desk, and the silver chain slithered in a pool around the rose scroll.

Disappointment dimmed the brightness of Renee's eyes. "You can't handle this alone, Alexa."

Beside the locket, I placed the Gotham Rose cell

phone, my connection to Alan's vast source of information, and made a mental note to pick up a replacement on my way back to the showgrounds.

"I never fit in, anyway."

I hurried back to the showgrounds, shaking all the way as I struggled to speed-learn the New York City subway system. I'd never taken public transportation before, and figuring out which way the trains went took a while to decipher.

The ride wasn't as bad as I'd imagined. Humidity did amplify the smells of hot bodies, cheap perfume and petroleum-scented recycled air. But I didn't feel threatened by any of the other passengers. My stop was only a few blocks away from Pier 94, and I made it back to the showgrounds in time for the lunch feed.

"Where have you been?" Dawn demanded as I strode toward Magnus's stall. "Ross was looking all over for you."

Had he figured out the connection between Karen Kallio's arrest and my presence here? I rubbed a circle over my stomach and made a face. "Bathroom. I think I got a bit of Erin's stomach bug."

Dawn's eyes nearly popped out of their sockets. "You missed all of the excitement."

"What happened?"

"Juliane's mother got arrested." Dawn savored each word as if she delighted in the family's distress.

"No!" I made my eyebrows shoot up in surprise. "For child abuse?"

"No, she's the Horse Ripper! The guys who arrested her were wearing NYPD and FBI jackets."

"You've got to be kidding. That small woman?"

"That *determined* woman."

"Well, if that's true, then we can all breathe a sigh of relief." For Magnus's sake, I hoped the real Horse Ripper wouldn't dare to strike now and throw the scent off Karen Kallio.

"Yeah, I suppose." Dawn's lips twitched. "They had Karen in handcuffs, and as they were dragging her away, she was screaming that she was going to sue the FBI, the NYPD and the mayor for false arrest. Flashes were going off all over the place. Her picture's going to be in all the papers! Probably the evening news, too."

Dawn's obvious reveling in other people's pain made me squirm with unease. "You said Ross was looking for me. Do you know where he is?"

"With Firewall." She shook her head. "He isn't looking good at all."

As I approached Firewall's stall, Ross stood facing the gelding. Firewall's eyes were half-closed and scrunched in pain.

"How's he doing?" I folded my arms over the top of the stall door and rested my chin on top of my hands.

"Looks like I'll have to put him down." Ross's rich voice bled with regret. He continued stroking the red horse's neck as if the touch of his big hands could ease Firewall's suffering.

White lines of defeat etched into Ross's face. For all his insistence that he never let himself care too much about anything, Firewall's condition was breaking his heart.

A hollow pit formed at the base of my stomach. "There must be something you can do."

"He's in pain."

"Surely VetTech has some product that could help him."

Ross shook his head. "The vet says there's nothing he can do to save Firewall."

"Don't you have anything at the experimental stage you could use?" The Governess had mentioned a research project involving ragwort weed. Not that I could mention that to Ross.

"Not for ragwort."

I reached over the door to touch his elbow, surprised by the overwhelming urge I had to revisit last night's scorching kiss. "I'm sorry, Ross. I know Firewall is a part of your dream. I know you're doing everything to save him."

"He's stopped eating. Look at him. He's so weak he can barely stand."

And it did seem as if all that was keeping Firewall upright was Ross's will. How would all this worry affect Magnus's big unveiling on Sunday? Magnus had to show.

I couldn't bear the thought of Firewall being put down. And I really wanted to believe Ross was on the good guys' side. That his hiding Magnus was to benefit those in need and not simply to line the coffers of his father's company. But I couldn't tell if I was letting my personal feelings color my judgment.

"Let me do a little research," I insisted. "Give me a couple of hours. I might find something. Please."

Ross shrugged, unconvinced. "His CGT level is 260."

A liver enzyme measure. Normal was somewhere between 0 and 87. Grim prospective, but Alan could help. He'd know where to look for an answer.

"Thanks," I said, taking his noncommittal answer as a yes. I wound my way to the food court for relative anonymity. Amid the din, someone would have to work hard to overhear my conversation. This new phone wasn't encrypted, but I didn't plan on staying on long. "Alan—"

I dug through my purse for the pad of paper I kept there.

"If you can save an Olympic champion, you'll be a hero. Firewall's vet says that ragwort poisoning is incurable. Could you ask your friend at Cornell—"

"Actually, I already have."

That's what I liked about Alan, he had a knack for knowing what you needed before you did. "And?"

"And there isn't anything allopathic medicine can do at this time."

Disappointment sank through me stone-hard. "No," I moaned.

"But there's a vet in England who's had good success using homeopathic medicine."

Hope, that's all I wanted to give Ross, a bit of hope to make him all the more determined to show Magnus on Sunday. "How can I get some of that?"

Alan hesitated.

"Please," I begged, the fingers of my right hand tight against the pen as I scoped the crowd milling around me.

He gave me the name and address of a local homeopathic vet as well as the prescription details of the cure the British vet had used.

"Thanks, Alan. I owe you one. If Renee gives you any grief, just blame it on me."

"I'll survive," he said, a note of pleasure tinkling through his voice. "Who else is Renee going to get to work my hours as cheerfully as I do?"

"You are one in a million."

"Go save that horse. Let me know the outcome."

"I will."

Passing myself off as Ross's assistant, I called Dr. Gerwitz right away and made arrangements for Firewall's care. Dr. Gerwitz would come for the horse himself, so he could keep him comfortable during the trailer ride. I figured with Ross's assets, money was no object, and if Firewall could be saved, the treatment would be worth every penny.

I rushed back to Firewall's stall to tell Ross about my findings. "There's a vet who's had great success in treating ragwort poisoning with homeopathic drugs. He's been able to lower the CGT levels within a month. And the horses have gone back to normal lives within six months." A setback for an Olympian, for sure, but a whole lot better than putting him to sleep.

"Homeopathy?" Ross's brows bunched with doubt. "Isn't that stuff kind of out there?"

"No more woo-woo than your sensoceuticals."

"That's science-based."

"But still unproven," I said, hiking up my chin. "You said you believed in miracles…"

Ross shook his head. "When I was a kid, I was sick a lot. I know what it's like to be helpless and in pain, and I don't want that for Firewall. If further tests and treatments aren't going to help him, I'd just as soon end his misery now."

At that moment, my heart softened. "If the treatment doesn't help, you can always change your mind."

I neglected to mention that Dr. Gerwitz had warned the first stages of detox could be horrifying to watch as the horse shivered and sweated out the poison. Another reason why I was so set on Firewall going to the clinic as soon as possible. Ross could focus on Magnus, and by the time he saw Firewall again, he'd be over the worst part. I tried to analyze why that seemed to matter so much to me.

"It's worth a shot, Ross. And there's a homeopathic vet not too far from the city. I have his name and number."

Firewall shuddered and rested his head on Ross's shoulder once more.

"Can you make the arrangements?"

"Already have. Dr. Gerwitz should be here in half an hour."

He arched a brow in surprise, then his eyes filled with a gratitude that made me wish for impossible things. He dropped a soft kiss on my cheek. "Thanks."

Heat poured into me. Oh, no. I was in deep trouble. If I wasn't careful, I could fall for him. Hard. And he didn't care for Alexa Cheltingham.

Ross leaned his cheek against Firewall's. "Then we'd better get Firewall ready to go."

The going was slow because Firewall was in so much pain, but we got him loaded in the vet's trailer. Ross insisted on traveling with him to settle him down. And I went back to work, keeping my eyes and ears peeled. Time slowed to a crawl, and watching and waiting thickened the air in my lungs until breathing was difficult.

I hadn't realized how much the invisible umbilical cord of the Rose Club's protection had provided me with a sense of security. I might have worked alone at the equestrian center and at the showgrounds, but I was still connected to help if I needed it.

I touched my throat and the empty space where the locket had lain and my heart clunked in my chest. I was on my own. No one to help.

The sounds of an argument, in low, scratchy voices, as if they feared being heard by others but still needed to express their ire, reached me and I went to investigate.

A man who looked as if he'd come out of central casting dressed for the role of Mafia thug—barrel-shaped with slicked-back hair and beady eyes pressed into a concrete-slab face—towered over Dawn in the feed stall.

"Get lost," Dawn said as she shoved the hay-filled wheelbarrow into his knees to get by.

"You're coming with me," Mafia Thug said, grabbing Dawn's elbow.

She prodded a nearby pitchfork at his chest. "I'm not going anywhere. I have work to do."

"This isn't a request. The boss wants to see you."

I frowned. The said boss couldn't be Richard Dunhill. Dealing with the help was Bart Hind's job. And brute force wasn't Hind's tactic of choice. The ten-thousand-dollar payment to Dawn's account popped into my mind. What was she selling and to whom?

"Then he can come here and talk to me," Dawn said with a touch of defiance.

"He" narrowed it down to half the population. I squeezed closer to the feed tent, ready to jump in if Dawn needed help.

"You missed the last meeting," Mafia Thug said. By the twist of pain on Dawn's face, I imagined that his grip on her elbow was vise tight.

"That's because I don't have anything." She yanked her imprisoned arm, but the man held on as if he wasn't even trying.

"This is your last chance." He let the words hang until their meaning hit home. "Show up or I can't guarantee your safety."

Dawn swallowed hard and let the pitchfork sag back to the ground. "When?"

"The party tonight. You'd better have something good."

"I've told you before. There's nothing. This is the last time."

"The boss calls time. Not you."

I grabbed a shovel, just in case, and drew closer. "Dawn is everything okay?"

"No, I'm fine. This bozo was just leaving."

The thug let go of her arm, but his narrowed glare bristled with warning. When he turned to look at me, his smile was sharp enough to make me cringe. "She's playing hard to get. All I wanted was a date."

"She's engaged," I said, and stood at her side, elbows splayed wide to make our combined mass appear bigger than it was. Not that it had a chance to fool the casting-central reject.

"Yeah, that's what I keep telling her." He winked

and made a gun with his fingers, then pulled an imaginary trigger. "Tonight. Don't be late."

Dawn watched him leave in stony silence.

"Who was that?" I asked.

She shook her head, her face as unreadable as a blank page. "Nobody important." She rolled the wheelbarrow to Loophole's stall. I followed her.

"Sounded important to me. And dangerous."

"I'm fine." She separated the hay bale into flakes and stuffed some into Loophole's net.

"Listen, Dawn," I pushed, "if you're in any danger, you need to speak up. We can help."

"I can handle him." She jerked a shoulder and averted her eyes. "He's just trying to intimidate me so I'll talk Todd out of pushing for a higher settlement. But, jeez, Todd was paralyzed, he should get enough to cover his care for the rest of his life."

She was lying. I could sense it as clearly as if her forehead bore a neon sign.

"You're not alone," I said. "If you need help, I'm here."

Her head tilted sideways. She pushed her glasses up her nose with a finger and studied me for a minute. "Thanks. That's nice to know."

"Are you going to meet him tonight?"

She honked as she closed Loophole's stall door. "No, I'm going to blow him off."

But the way she licked her lips and nervously glanced at her watch made me think otherwise.

"I'm glad," I said. "That guy looked like bad news. I think you should let the police take care of him. Last time I checked, blackmail was illegal."

"When there's a lot of money at stake, people tend to skirt the law." Dawn rolled the wheelbarrow toward Double Vision's stall, putting an end to the conversation.

I turned back to Magnus's stall, unable to shake the feeling that Dawn was in over her head in something serious. And if she was selling information, she could be in touch with the real Horse Ripper.

I glanced at my watch. The exhibitors' party started at seven. I planned on being there to see who Dawn was meeting.

Chapter 12

I arrived at the party early to find an inconspicuous corner from where I could keep an eye out for Dawn and her mysterious boss. The food court—officially known as The Tavern Courtyard Café—was already crowded.

This party wasn't a fund-raiser for charity, but a way for competitors to let off a little steam. The venue also wasn't ritzy. Layers of gold and green tablecloths and bouquets of gold and green balloons disguised the tables. Music pumped from a band that could turn everything from Gershwin to Green Day into elevator music. A few brave souls dared the dance floor. Mostly people stood in clusters, no doubt speculating about Karen Kallio's arrest.

Everyone wore half masks that covered the tops of their faces—mine was a simple black one—and figuring who was who kept me on edge and made me wish I had a pair of eyes on the back of my head.

I spied Claudine hobbling with a cane because of her sprained ankle from that morning's fall. Through her shiny gold mask, she searched for Roman who sat at a table at the far end of the room with a blonde on each knee. He hadn't bothered with a mask. Claudine's mouth flattened with cold fury when she spotted him with his tongue halfway down a competitor's throat.

I pretended to ponder the choices on the hors d'oeuvre table while I kept an eye out for Dawn. She arrived, wearing a red-and-black harlequin mask. Her eyes darted and her face twitched as she looked around. She parked by the bar and knocked back drinks as if they were water.

Leah Siegel sidled to the table, looking as if she'd rather be back with Waldo than here in this crowd. She'd chosen a mask with pale blue feathers that spoked out from a catlike black base, but her strawberry-blond ponytail and her shy manners gave her away.

"Some party," I said.

"Yes."

I plucked a stuffed mushroom from a silver platter. "These are great."

"Um, okay, I'll try one, then."

"Waldo looked good at practice this morning."

Her whole body brightened at the mention of her horse. "He's doing so well. It's like he can read my mind."

"I think it's all the time you spend with him that makes the difference."

"And not having to worry about the Horse Ripper hurting him. Can you believe Karen Kallio would do something like that?"

"People do strange things. I read about a mother who hired a hitman to kill her daughter's cheerleading competitor just so her daughter could have a spot on the team."

Leah shook her head as she added a miniquiche to her plate. "That's so crazy. How did she think she was going to get away with it? And I'm sure her daughter isn't thanking her for the scandal. Imagine showing your face at school after people find out?"

"I guess that's why Juliane scratched from the show."

"I can't blame her. I'd be mortified if my father did anything like that."

Just then Mayor Siegel walked through the entrance, paused in a pose that reminded me of Alfred Hitchcock's silhouette on my friend Nat's DVDs— round belly, prominent chin and nose. He zoomed in on his daughter and strolled toward her, pumping hands as he went.

"How's my girl?" he asked, clasping an arm around Leah's bowed shoulders.

"Daddy, I didn't expect to see you here."

"Well, I figured I'd put in an appearance and make sure everyone is having a good time."

Leah turned to include me in the conversation. "Daddy, this is Ally. She takes care of Waldo for me."

"Pleased to meet you, young lady." He joggled my hand with a politician's glee. "My daughter's happy at the Ashcroft Equestrian Center."

Pinky in the air, he snapped a stuffed mushroom from Leah's plate and closed his eyes as it slid down his throat. "So you're going to make me proud and win on Sunday?"

"I'll do my best." She moved the miniquiche and the Swedish meatball around her plate as if they were chess pieces.

"Can't ask for more. It's not often I get to see my girl jumping right in my own backyard and get to show her off to all my friends."

Which included all the who's who of New York society. Somehow I had a feeling Leah found it more relaxing to show anywhere but this city. How much pressure was her father putting on her?

The mayor steered Leah toward the crowd. "You can't hide here all evening. Let me introduce you to a few people." He turned to me and smiled, showing off his perfectly bleached teeth. "I hope you have a delightful evening."

"Thank you, Mr. Mayor."

Somehow I doubted he'd have dismissed Alexa

Cheltingham that easily. Not that I had time for chit-chat right now.

Dawn hadn't moved from the bar. If she kept up this pace much longer, she'd keel over before her "boss" made an appearance.

"You clean up good." Ross's voice rippled behind me as rich and as silky as a dark-chocolate fountain, ruffling a wave of pleasure down my spine.

I whirled around to face him. Oh, my. So did he. Like his brother, he wore no mask. Lines of fatigue webbed Ross's eyes, but his broad shoulders showed off the blue Prada shirt to perfection.

"How did Firewall fare with the trailer ride?"

"He was tired," Ross said, making me want to kiss away the sadness in his voice. "But the calmer environment seemed to do him some good right away. He's resting comfortably. Dr. Gerwitz is going to start the treatment in the morning."

I squeezed his hand. "Everything's going to turn out fine."

He twisted my palm around until my hand was trapped in his and our fingers intertwined. "If it does, I'll have you to thank."

My face flooded with heat and I jerked a shoulder. "All I did was make a few phone calls."

Before I quite knew how it happened, we were on the dance floor, swaying to a vapid rendition of Velvet Revolver's "Fall to Pieces." I tried to keep Dawn in sight, but Ross pulled me close, his big hands palming my waist possessively. The leather and musk of his aftershave and his heat wrapped around me, closing off the rest of the room. I was feeling another meltdown coming on. Once was bad enough.

I splayed a hand flat against his chest. "Not a good idea."

He leaned his head against mine, trapping my hand against his heart, the strong pulse beating right into my palm. "I think it's a perfect idea."

"I have a rule. I never date people I work with. Or for."

"Um," he said as he skimmed a hand up and down my back, setting off minifirecrackers along my spine. Oh, my. With hands like that, no wonder he was such a good rider. I arched my back, into his hot palm. "Maybe you won't need to work much longer."

"Ross—"

He stopped my protest with a kiss. An all-consuming invasion—as if the heat he generated could vaporize all of the despair Firewall's condition had caused. The music seemed to fall inside me, and my blood pulsed to the strumming guitar. My heart jolted into a crazy little dance that made me wonder at my sanity.

He released my mouth and rested his clean-shaven cheek against mine. His hot, rapid breaths labored against my ear. The hardness of his erection pressed a dent against the fly of my good jeans. Running his fingers through my hair, he lifted my head and looked at me with pupils wide open, as if the incendiary chemistry between us had singed him.

That look made me feel feminine and pretty…normal, in a way I'd never felt. He wanted me and he wasn't faking.

"Let's get out of here," he whispered in a thick voice. Oh, yes. I definitely wanted more of this. He grabbed my hand and my feet tracked right along his long stride.

We were just out of the café area, when he crashed me into an alcove and kindled another scorching kiss.

His big hands plunged under my one good shirt and skimmed my breasts. I gasped and pulled his shirttail from his pants. Kissing him like someone starving, I pressed my hands on his tight abs, feeling the fiery heat of his skin set mine on fire.

His hands coasted down my ribs and cupped my buttocks, lifting me off the ground. I wound my legs around him, reveling in the sweet friction of his hips against mine. All I could think about was feeling his skin against mine. Until his hand slid down my thigh and reality knocked some sense into me.

My leg.

I froze.

Would he turn from me in disgust? He didn't think much of Alexa Cheltingham and her Park Avenue ways. I had to tell him who I was before he saw my leg.

His fingers came perilously close to my socket. Heart beating out of time, I unwound my legs from around his hips and slid until my toes touched the ground. Had he noticed the hard steel of my work-out leg?

"Ally," he said, his voice breathy, needy. "What's wrong?"

Even as my head spun and my mind searched for words, I caught sight of Dawn being yanked toward the entrance by Mafia Thug's bigger twin.

"I…I have to go," I said, gripping the expensive material of his shirt, strangely reluctant to let go. "I'm sorry."

I spun out of his embrace. As the band's lead singer crooned about being all alone and falling to pieces, I cut across the aisle to where I'd seen Dawn disappear, leaving Ross staring after me.

Body shaking from the close call with disaster with Ross, I searched for Dawn and Mafia Thug Two. The harsh light threw everything in sharp contrast, making the concrete glare and the shadows along the edge deep.

"I told you. There's nothing to tell."

Dawn's voice. Loud and not quite steady against the fading thump of the band's bass.

I hurried to the far aisle of the stall area and peeked around the corner to see Mafia Thug Two dragging Dawn toward the far end of the aisle. At the other end of the building there was a storage area where no unauthorized personnel were supposed to enter—making it a perfect spot for a thug who wanted some serious one-on-one time with a reluctant snitch.

As I cautiously followed, everything felt wrong. The air was too thick. Horse sounds too sharp. The blast of the air conditioner too cold. I wished I hadn't left the locket on Renee's desk, that I still was connected to help with the press of one button. At least I still had a cell phone.

Thug Two jerked Dawn into a sharp turn at the entrance to the wash stalls. What else was back there? The HVAC center. Plenty of noise from the machinery keeping the place heated, ventilated and air-conditioned to drown out tortured cries.

I crept around the corner and stepped onto Dawn's fallen mask, cracking the brittle red-and-black plastic in two. A rush of adrenaline flooded my system, spurring my pulse into a reckless gallop. Holding my breath, I scanned the area, but no other thug slunk out of the woodwork.

The guy mauling Dawn was big. The number-one tactic Jimmy had pounded into our brains was to avoid confrontation, that our feet running in the opposite direction was our best weapon. But I couldn't very well let Dawn get beaten up—or worse.

I slipped my cell phone out of my pocket and started to dial 911 only to have the thing ripped out of my hand by the original Mafia Thug.

"I don't think so," he said, and stepped on the phone with his eelskin cowboy boot, cracking it into a hundred jagged pieces. His other hand held a knife—one with a mean blade that looked as if it could butcher a hog in less than five minutes. "You're coming with me."

"I don't think so." I whipped off my mask and threw it at him. He flinched, batted away the plastic and came at me. In one swift move, I turned so that my body was no longer in the flight path of his knife and thrust a fist to his face, breaking his nose. Blood flowed. He fell back onto his can, a shocked expression on his face. Before he could rise, I stomped on his wrist, forcing him to let go of the knife.

The metal clattered against the concrete floor, echoing in the wide space. He tried to rise, but like a dervish, I kept hammering him with kicks to the hands and face until he passed out.

Puffing, I dragged him into a wash stall and trussed him up with a hose and snatched up his knife.

Inside the HVAC room, Dawn's shrill screams pierced the din of pumping machinery. Her glasses lay broken on the ground. "I don't know anything! Please, stop. I don't know anything. She does. She'll tell you."

"I don't want excuses." In the dim light, I could barely make out Thug Two as his meaty punches smacked against Dawn's face. "I paid for results."

Armed with Thug One's knife, I braced for assault. "Let her go."

With a whack across Dawn's temple, Thug Two

let her drop. She lay there dazed for a second, then scrambled blindly under a fat duct close to the ground.

"You should learn to mind your own business, girlie." He flicked open a jackknife and came at me. My nerves jangled like a full carillon of bells. Gaze fixed on Thug Two, I edged toward Dawn.

He cut me off with a, "Nah-uh. I'm not done with her."

"Dawn, run for help."

He came at me, thrusting the knife at my chest. I deflected its course with an upward jab that skimmed the edge of his blade against the side of my palm like a stinging paper cut. I didn't want to kill him; that would make things too complicated. So I jabbed the tip of the blade into the nerves of his wrist and sliced. He dropped the knife.

I crammed the butt of my weapon into his nose, fracturing it and jammed my heel into his instep. For good measure, I kneed him in the groin. As he staggered back, howling in pain, I lunged for Dawn. But he pounced on me and nearly squished me flat with his weight, dislodging my weapon.

Screaming to free myself from paralysis, I kicked and punched with everything I had, rolling him off me. I rocked onto my rear and let fly a series of ax kicks. I spun onto one side, using my heels to rake and crush his head and torso until he stopped fighting and lay there, face scraped raw and shirt shredded.

Breathless, I lurched to my feet, grabbed both knives, then Dawn's arm, sticking out from under the duct, dragged her out and staggered back into the main aisle with her. "Help!" I screamed. "Help!"

A hired security guard came around the corner, firearm drawn.

"Someone attacked my friend," I said. "Call the police. There're two big guys in the wash stalls."

The guard flipped open his cell phone to call the cops.

"They're on their way," he said. "You two okay?"

"We're okay."

"Stick around for the cops."

"No," Dawn begged, so low I could barely hear her. "No cops. That'll only make things worse."

"Someone attacked you."

Tears mixed with the blood on her face. "Please." She attempted to fight her way out of my support and teetered against a stall door. The horse occupying the space scrambled back and snorted. "No cops. No cops."

Why didn't she want to call the cops? "Those thugs almost killed you."

"No cops." Her fear was so strong it emitted a fetid smell.

"Okay." Pocketing both knives, I kept alert for a chance to slip away. "At least let me help you."

Nodding, she deflated against me. "Just get me out of here."

I managed to ease her into the next aisle and down

to our tent area. I sat her down in the director's chair in the tack room, hid the knives at the bottom until I could decide what to do with them, wishing I still had use of Alan's services, then plucked the first-aid kit from the equipment locker.

"Are you all right?" Her bottom lip was split and swollen. Her eyes and cheeks were purpling fast. Tears gushed freely, streaking blood down her face as if she were a two-year-old who'd played with her mother's lipstick. "Maybe we should get you to a hospital."

"I'm screwed." She rubbed at the doorknob-size knot on her head. "I'm so screwed."

"The cops can help."

She shook her head. "Too late."

"It's never too late." I plucked an ice pack and a bottle of water from the small fridge. I fitted the ice pack to her hand and pressed it against the knot on her head. I poured water from the bottle onto a stack of gauze squares and dabbed at the blood on her face. "Come on, tell me about it."

Her head hung to her chest, accepting defeat. "All I wanted was something of my own."

"Everybody's entitled to a dream."

"A little piece of land, Todd, a couple of kids, a couple of horses."

"That's a good dream, Dawn." I reached for clean gauze and continued to wipe the blood from her face.

"Then Todd got hurt."

"And you have the settlement coming to seed your dream."

"Now, yes, but not then. The farm was balking. They didn't want to pay. It looked like his case was going to be tied up in court for years. So when they promised me Todd could walk again, what could I do?"

Walk again? "They who?"

"I don't know."

"What do you mean you don't know?"

"They always tell you that if it sounds too good to be true, then it is." She snorted, bubbling snot. "I should've known. The nerves are severed. He'll never walk again. But I wanted to believe."

"Of course you did," I said in soothing tones as I applied antibiotic cream to her cuts. Ross's project. She had to be talking about Ross's project. Had a competing company paid her to spy on Ross so they could steal the technology he'd used to heal Magnus? Did Dawn know who Magnus really was?

Dawn dropped the hand holding the ice pack to her head into her lap. "So I said yes."

"To what?"

She swallowed hard and made a noise deep in her throat that sounded like a dying animal.

I crouched beside her and touched her hand. "I can't help you if I don't know what's going on."

"It doesn't matter anyway. They don't believe me. I don't know anything and they don't believe me."

"Don't know anything about what?"

She looked at me, eyes creased with fresh pain. "You're not safe, either."

"Safe from what?"

"You're being so nice and I—I—" Her mouth stayed open, but no sound came out.

"Safe from what?" I pushed.

"From the bozos." Snot ran from her nose and she wiped it with the back of her hand. "I told the big one you'd know."

"Know what?"

Her laugh was crazed. "That's just it. I don't know. Whatever they want. I'm sorry. I'm so sorry."

What had she tangled me in? My gut tightened. I wanted to shake her. "What were you supposed to do for them?"

"Let them know everything Ross did."

"And?"

"And that's it." Dawn turned over the ice pack in her lap. "Ross is one of the good guys. He rides and works and he's nice to everyone. Even the grooms. They thought he had something, but I never found anything."

I breathed a sigh of relief. If she thought riding Magnus late at night and asking Mandy for help was something out of the ordinary, she hadn't mentioned it to the thugs. Magnus was still safe.

"Was Mandy your source of information?"

She nodded. "Ross took her out to dinner a few times to talk about the horses. She'd tell me what they talked about and I'd tell them."

"That's why you got paid ten thousand dollars?"

Her eyes widened, but she didn't question how I knew about the money. "After Bandit got hit by the Ripper, I heard an argument between Roman and Ross, about the horse show and how everything was going to come out then. I was supposed to find out more details."

Why hadn't I overheard that argument? "What was going to come out?" I asked, even though I already knew the answer. Ross would reveal Magnus's real identity and the success of Hardel Industries' secret project.

"I don't know. They didn't say."

"Where did this argument take place? At the equestrian center?"

She shook her head. "At the bank. I was getting some money out of the ATM for the trip and they were outside in the parking lot."

I'd heard Ross and Roman disagree over business, too. "And you don't know who this person is who wants this information on Ross?"

"No idea. It just seemed like an easy way to make money so Todd and I could be together. And bozo said that if I got him the right information, it could mean Todd would walk again."

I questioned Dawn for a few more minutes, but I'd tapped her shallow well of information, and she was fading fast. She still refused to go to the hospital, so I called around and checked her into another hotel in case the thugs knew where she was staying.

After taking a shower, swallowing aspirin, bandaging the cut on my hand, icing my multiplying bruises and changing clothes, I headed back to the showgrounds to spend what was left of the night in Magnus's stall.

Ross and I needed to talk about what had happened between us, but I wasn't quite ready to have him know Alexa Cheltingham was playing groom to his horses. Not until I understood if the thugs who had attacked Dawn were a danger to Magnus. I unhooked my leg for comfort, but left it in the jeans leg in case I needed to act fast.

To get to Magnus, the thugs would have to go through me.

Chapter 13

News of the murder reached the showgrounds before the crime scene was even cordoned off.

The buzz started at the front gate and spread furiously until it reached the far end of the stall area. I'd stuffed the last hay net when the day-shift guard arrived to take over from the night-shift guy, talking about how a groom was found with her throat slit from ear to ear in her hotel room.

A feeling of dread swamped over me, and nausea slithered in my stomach. Dawn.

Both thugs last night had come equipped with sharp knives. Thug Two had said he wasn't finished with her. Even if *he* was still in jail, there could be more central-casting rejects where he'd come from.

And Dawn hadn't shown that morning.

I thought she was in too much pain to move, so I'd made excuses for her absence and told everyone she had a hangover. I was going to check on her at lunch and bring her some food. Now I had a terrible feeling I was too late. I shouldn't have listened to her last night. I should've made her call the cops and get protection.

"What happened?" I asked the guard, closing the door to Magnus's stall with extra care.

He hiked up his pants and cleared his throat. "The maid found her. Lying in a pool of her own blood, she was. They say the cut was so deep her—"

"That's horrible." I held on to my stomach before it heaved. "Who was it?"

His right hand touched his holster. "Don't know. One of the girls grooming for the show."

"Which hotel?" My heart sank when he named Dawn's. How had they found her? I'd checked her in under an alias and paid cash.

I hurried through my chores and looked for Erin who was cleaning tack. "I'm going to check on Dawn. I'll be right back."

I'd told her an edited version of Dawn's attack last night to explain her lateness. Erin had heard the rumors flying. She opened her mouth, closed it and nodded, concentrating on polishing the bit as if it was caked with a year's worth of slobber.

She wanted to know, too, but like me, dreaded the answer.

The hotel was crawling with cops, and getting to Dawn's floor required multiple proofs of identity. I gasped when I saw Dawn's room door open. The coppery smell of blood tainted the air. Police radios crackled with unintelligible chatter. A raw tension crazed the atmosphere. I forced myself to keep walking.

One of the cops eyed me suspiciously and raised a hand to stop me. "No one's allowed on this floor."

I showed him my key card and pointed to my door. "That's my room."

"You'll have to leave till we clear the scene."

"My friend wasn't feeling well. Dawn Waller. Is she okay?"

"Sorry, kid."

My hands were shaking so hard I dropped my key card to the floor. As I bent to pick it up, I got a full view of the second bed. A knife was jammed to the hilt into the pillow. A halo of blood had seeped from the blade into the white pillowcase. Dawn's blood. No need to wait for forensics to know.

This was a message.

If I'd slept in that bed last night, I'd be dead, too.

I must have gasped because the cop who'd told me to leave was now calling for the detectives.

Once the police were through questioning me at the hotel, I hurried back to the showgrounds. Not that

I remember how I got there, because all I could see was that bloody knife in my pillow.

Killing Dawn for not knowing the information the thugs wanted seemed rather harsh—and not very practical. If they killed her, they killed their spy. She'd lied to me yesterday—more than once. What was she hiding?

After checking on Magnus, I went through Dawn's belongings in the dressing room and tack room. My hands still shook from the residual shock as I hunted for Todd's phone number or an address. The police had asked for his last name and I hadn't known it.

In all the mess of discarded food wrappers and tools in Dawn's things, I couldn't find an address book or see anything worth killing her over. At the bottom of her grooming tote, I found half of a photograph.

I sagged onto a tack trunk and studied the picture showing a woman with a young boy. No family resemblance—which didn't necessarily mean anything. Both the woman and the child appeared to be Latino. The palm trees, mountains and architecture of the house suggested a South American location. Mexico? Farther south? A masculine hand rested on the young boy's shoulder, but the man was missing, ripped away. In anger?

The caption on the back read, "with Julio and Maricela Vitiello." Why would Dawn have this photograph? Why would she keep it in a dirty place like the bottom of a grooming kit?

I slipped the photograph in my jeans pocket and let the questions stew inside my mind. Even though Renee had pulled me from the case, she needed to see this photograph and to hear about Dawn's murder and her spying activities.

Which meant I couldn't tell Ross who I was yet. Even though I was no longer an agent, I couldn't ever tell him about my involvement with the Gotham Rose Club, either. And Ross would want answers. I'd come up with something when the time came.

Ross was with Magnus when I approached his stall. I gripped the cold metal tubing of the stall door. The memory of his searing kisses and heated hands on my skin flared in full IMAX 3-D splendor, and warmth rushed to all the wrong places as our gazes met.

He started to reach out to me, then swerved his hand to Magnus. Okay, I deserved that for leaving him standing there last night with a hard-on and no explanation.

He gave me a stiff nod.

I cleared my throat. "Look, things got complicated last night. You probably think I'm a jerk for leaving when things got, um, hot, but I was worried about Dawn. She looked like she was in trouble and needed a friend—"

"You left because Dawn was in trouble?" Disbelief charged his every word.

I risked a touch to his elbow, but he jerked away from it. "Dawn was found dead this morning in her hotel." My throat worked hard at the memory of the blood. "Someone slit her throat." I left out the detail of the knife in my pillow.

"Are you okay?" Ross asked. He eyed me up and down as if to reassure himself that I was. I could take care of myself, but it was nice to know someone else cared.

I nodded, looking everywhere but at his too-sharp gaze. "It's so awful. Why would someone want to kill Dawn?"

"I don't know." But he brushed Magnus with strokes that were too quick, causing the horse to flinch. "Todd will be devastated. She was the one giving him hope for the future. Have the police contacted the family?"

"I'm not sure, but other than Todd, I don't think she had anyone."

"That's rough." He dropped the brush in the brush caddy, then stalked out of Magnus's stall. Next thing I knew, he'd grasped my shoulders. "You're fired."

"What?" I pulled back, breaking his hold. "You can't fire me. I don't work for you."

"I don't want you here."

"You don't get a vote."

"It's too dangerous. I don't want to see you hurt."

I looked into his beautiful face and the internal battle waging itself in his eyes. "This is because of Magnus, isn't it? The Horse Ripper. Dawn. Somehow it's all connected to you and VetTech." I purposefully left out Roman's name.

"I don't know. Not for sure."

"Dawn's dead, Ross. Maybe she was working with Karen Kallio and maybe Karen had her silenced so she couldn't talk."

His gaze narrowed as he silently gauged me to see how much I knew. "Maybe."

I really wanted to slug him. Here I'd been contemplating bearing my soul—and my residual limb—to him and he didn't trust me. With all I'd gone through to protect his horses, he still didn't trust me. So what the hell was that pawing session all about last night?

I had a sick feeling I knew. And he wasn't going to lay his cards on the table. Fine by me.

My chin cranked up. "Get this straight. I'm staying for Magnus. I'll be damned if I'm going to let anything happen to him after what happened to Bandit and Firewall."

"Even Magnus isn't worth your life."

But what his healing represented could help so many. "I can take care of myself. So you're stuck with me until the show's over."

"Why are you doing this?" He seemed about to add something, then clamped his mouth shut.

"Because I love horses," I huffed, exasperated at proving myself. And, damn it, I'd accepted an assignment. I was going to see it through all the way and accept the consequences of my decisions.

His expression turned grim. "No more heroics. Let the police handle the bad guys."

"Whatever you say." The client was always right and it wasn't my fault the police were never around when I needed help. I brushed past Ross. "Show day's tomorrow and I have a lot to do."

I spent the rest of the day alternating between answering more questions from the detectives and bathing and trimming Trademark, Waldo and Magnus.

I didn't let Magnus out of my sight or anyone get close to his stall. I wasn't going to take any chances. At eleven, I bedded down in Magnus's stall.

An hour later, footsteps approached. I snapped my leg on, ready to fight the intruder.

The steps slowed, then became stealthy. The light in the aisleway caused the figure bent over the door latch to appear in silhouette.

Heart thumping hard, I prepared to jump. Then I recognized Ross's clean saddle and musk scent. "Ross? What are you doing here?"

"Same as you by the looks of it."

He entered Magnus's stall, carrying a couple of blankets. Magnus checked Ross's pockets for a treat. After gobbling down a sugar cube, he went back to his hay. Ross spread one of the blankets on the shavings, then sat and patted the space beside him. "Might as well get comfy. It's going to be a long night."

I eyed him suspiciously. "I'm fine where I am, thanks." To prove it, I yawned.

"Suit yourself."

I leaned back against the stall wall and forced my

eyes closed. In a few hours, I'd have to get up and start braiding. And that should be a real treat considering I wasn't quite sure how to achieve the job. I hadn't planned on actually sleeping, but I must have dozed off. When I opened my eyes, Ross was snoring gently beside Magnus.

I watched over the two beautiful creatures until it was time to get to work.

On Sunday morning, while the horses munched on their hay, I braided Trademark's and Magnus's manes.

"I'll do Waldo next," I said to Leah when she arrived.

"I'll braid him myself. It helps settle my nerves."

Which was just as well because my fingers were stiff, throbbing and raw by the time I'd done two manes and the braids were on the rough side. Roman would complain.

My head pounded and my body ached in ways I'd never imagined. My back and leg muscles were stiff from yet another night spent on a wood-shaving mattress. And standing on a milk crate for hours wasn't exactly the best thing for my leg.

One more day, I told myself. A few more hours and it would be all over. I hoped.

Ross or I stayed glued to Magnus's side all morning.

Four hours to show time, I fed the horses a light meal of hay and made sure their coats shone. My nerves were stretched taut, making me aware of every little noise around me. As I pinned Ross's number to his jacket, I wished we'd met again under different circumstances. I wasn't looking forward to telling him who I really was.

Two hours before show time, I tacked Trademark and Magnus and walked them to the ring so Grant could warm them up.

Counting down to show time, the riders walked the course with Grant to figure out pacing and plot personal strategies. Claudine joined them, announcing she'd spent the morning getting a facial and massage to rejuvenate herself.

"I thought you'd decided to scratch," Grant asked.

"No, it's just a sprain," Claudine said. "I should be able to ride."

I was sure she'd use her sprained ankle as an excuse for her inability to ride a clean round. She was such a fake.

The course consisted of thirteen brightly colored fences. The 490 yard course was demanding. The riders would have to think fast and react quickly to complete it under the allotted seventy-two seconds. Clean rounds were a priority.

Sparks, like electricity, energized the air. The backstage area and the stands swarmed with activity. Television cameras panned the crowd, seeking out celebrities. The Diamond Circle was filled with society's upper crust dressed to the nines in diamonds and couture. Crystal, china and silver graced their five-thousand-dollar tables.

An hour before the class, Ross changed into his show clothes. Snow-white breeches, a crisp white shirt and a gold-lined navy jacket had never looked so fine.

"Are you sure you want to do this?" I asked as I handed Magnus to Ross in the warm-up ring.

"Absolutely. There's too much at stake to back down now."

I nodded and let him go, but kept a hawk's eye on them. Who knew what the Horse Ripper might decide to do? Especially when backed into a do-or-die corner like this with billions of dollars at stake.

When the riders came out of the schooling ring to head into the show ring and chill out a few minutes before their names were called, I was ready with my kit for last minute touch-ups.

"Hoof oil," Roman demanded as he brought Trademark to a sharp halt. I painted shiny black goo on Trademark's hooves, then toweled off the arena dust from Roman's boots. I did the same for Ross and Leah.

As they entered the staging area, a grooming tote lay in the middle of the way. A bomb? Cautiously I approached the abandoned tote. With a hoof pick from my kit, I inspected the contents.

"Hey! What are you doing?" A frantic-looking girl, wearing a multipocketed apron, swooped up the tote. "That's mine."

"Sorry, I thought it might be a bomb."

She shook her head as if I were nuts. "My rider's horse was acting up. I left it for a second. No need to make a federal case out of it."

"No problem," I said, backing away, hands up in surrender. I trotted up to wait with Ross and guard Magnus.

The announcer's voice boomed over the PA system. "Our next rider is Leah Siegel, riding her chestnut, Dutch warmblood gelding, Waldo. This is her first competition since her back injury last fall. Let's see if she can pick up her hot streak where she left off."

The ring steward opened the in gate, allowing Leah into the arena.

Eyes wide, she swallowed hard as she cued Waldo into a canter. She glanced over to the Diamond Circle where her father sat, a king surrounded by his court.

The electronic starter gonged, setting the clock on the giant scoreboard in motion. Waldo understood the meaning of that sound and added more spring to his step. Over the first fence, a vertical, Leah looked tense. By the end of the round, she'd knocked down three fences and acquired a total of twelve faults.

I rushed to meet her at the gate, but as she vaulted off, she said, "That's okay. I've got him." And looked relieved that her ordeal was over for the day. So was I. I wanted to stick close to Magnus.

Claudine ended her round with a refusal and time faults. Roman's ride was rough, but in show jumping, style didn't count—only jumping clean and fast—and he'd jumped clean.

Ross was next. As the ring steward called him in, Ross bent over Magnus's neck, petting him. "This is it, boy. Show time."

The gong went off and Magnus transformed into a living sculpture with his sinewy muscles rippling, prominent veins pumping blood and flaring nostrils drinking in oxygen. As he reached the first vertical, he stretched his neck, tucked his knees and seemed to suspend in air for a few seconds before clearing the fence. His hooves stabbed the ground on his way to the next fence.

Ross rode brilliantly, and Magnus made each jump look as if it was meant for a pony class. With a final burst of speed, they blasted toward the finish line. I held my breath until the timer stopped. Then, to the thunder of the crowd's applause, I ran to meet them at the gate.

"You did it! You did it!" I said, grinning like a fool.

Ross's smile captured a world of pride—not at his own riding ability, but at his horse's performance. "We made it through the first round."

After the first round, only three competitors remained. Roman, Ross and Isabella Madderley, a surprise contender on her Selle Français, Tiger Lily. The jump-off would consist of seven fences. If there was a tie, whoever had gone over the course in the fastest time would win.

A horse kicked against the wood boards of the arena and a crack, as sharp as a shotgun's retort, reminded me that the danger to Magnus wasn't over yet. Someone still had time to bring him down, and with him, Ross's project that could help so many.

"Don't hurry," Grant said to Ross as they went over their strategy for the next round. "The line is easy."

"We're not in a hurry." Standing beside Magnus, Ross petted his horse's neck. Magnus blew his agreement into Ross's dark brown hair and I felt a twinge too near to jealousy at the closeness of their relationship. *You are definitely going crazy, Alexa.*

I scanned the crowd. Purses, flowy ponchos and hats all became places to hide a weapon. The bursts of laughter, the buzzing din of constant conversation, the clack of steel studs against concrete became the sounds of possible bullets aiming for Magnus.

My nerves were like bacon on a griddle and I wanted the heat turned off.

"Take the long approach to the first jump to start him off feeling relaxed." Grant swiped at the sweat beading his brow. "You can cut a stride between eight and nine. But turning over the oxer might cause him to hit the fence."

"I'm planning to ride, not rush," Ross said.

"You've still got the clock to worry about. Work with him, but don't let him get too excited."

"He's having a blast."

Grant's face turned gloomy. "Stay focused. You have to stay focused if you're going to win."

Ross's smile broadened as he knuckled Magnus on the muzzle and rubbed. "Magnus is already a winner. I'm not doing this for anyone but him."

I don't know what it was about those words that jolted through me like an electric shock. I gasped, and Ross skewed a grin at me over his shoulder.

"Don't worry," he said. "We're going to give a win our best shot."

I nodded distractedly.

I'm not doing this for anyone but him.

Roman hated riding, but rode because his father was there today, sitting between Mayor Siegel and Ryan Green, the real estate developer. Roman didn't seem to know about the project, about Magnus. And he was desperate to impress his father. Was he desperate enough to bring down Magnus just because he was Ross's mount and Roman needed this win…if for nothing else than as a negotiation tool in this unbalanced father-son triangle?

I scoured the milling crowd, searching for Roman. Where was he? Why wasn't he with Grant and Ross getting some last-minute advice from his trainer?

I spotted him and Claudine near the schooling ring, exchanging verbal blows that packed a punch.

I ran a towel over Ross's boots and said, "I'll be right back."

Tote in hand, I headed toward Roman and Claudine. Neither looked particularly happy. Roman's rage-reddened skin showed through his tan, and Claudine's hushed but sharp words could slice leather without effort. A frown cut deep lines in her forehead, as she leaned heavily on her cane with one hand and white-knuckled Trademark's reins in the other.

"I had five seconds over him," Roman snarled. The win meant a lot to him. This was as close as he'd gotten in the past two seasons to besting his brother.

"That's not good enough," Claudine insisted, pulling on Trademark's rein as if she could bring Roman down to her level. "What if he's faster this time?"

Roman shrugged. "He's going to take the easy lines. He always does."

No doubt about it, they were talking about Ross. But it didn't sound as if Roman was the evil twin I'd made him out to be. Could he possibly want to win fair and square?

Listening to Roman vent his frustration to Claudine, I heard all the self-doubt I'd kept hidden inside me over the years. Doubts fed by my parents—and even Renee and the Governess. Why was it that you always had to be somebody different to be liked?

Roman couldn't win in the arena chosen by his father, so he was judged less. Claudine couldn't measure up in her father's eyes, so she was trying to get to her destination of social clout by using someone else. Were these empty ambitions they'd never reach?

Which had me wondering why I was knocking my head so hard against the wall to prove myself to the Gotham Rose Club.

Like a rabid dog, Claudine turned on me as I approached. "What do you want?"

I aimed my answer at Roman. "I just wanted to see if you needed anything before you went back in."

Roman's mouth stretched in what passed for a smile. "Claudine's playing groom for me this round."

"Okay," I said, and pointed toward Ross and Grant. "I'll be right over there if you need me."

He nodded, and they both waited for me to leave.

"It's time," Claudine said, her words barely audible in the babel of surrounding conversation. "I'll be back for Ross's round. You'll win. I promise."

I didn't like the sound of that.

Claudine dropped the reins, then hobbled away with her cane. I stashed my tote by the box office booth and hurried after as she headed toward the vendor area.

The place was crawling with gawkers who clogged the aisles, making footing for my prosthesis precarious. A shock of color exploded from each booth. Voices echoed in a dull roar in the warehouselike building.

Claudine used her cane to clear a path for herself. I followed, unable to avoid bumping into people as I struggled to keep her in sight. She was just one salon blonde in a sea of salon blondes.

Then she slipped between two tents. By the time I reached the narrow aisleway, she'd disappeared.

Chapter 14

I couldn't do this alone. There were too many people and too many places for Claudine to hide. I would need a whole team of people to do this right. Then I spotted Erin standing in line at the food court and grabbed her. An extra pair of eyes was better than nothing.

"I need help," I said.

"What's wrong?" Erin glanced back with longing at the burger stand.

"Claudine is going to try to hurt Magnus so Roman can win, and I need to stop her. I lost her in this crowd. I have to find her before Ross starts his round."

"I wouldn't put anything past her," Erin said with a sour-lemon face. "That watch she accused me of stealing? It was in her purse the whole time. Where'd you last see her?"

"Going around the corner between the needle-point tent and the silversmith tent."

Erin frowned. "The bathrooms, the coat checks and the show office are off that way."

My heart skipped a beat every time I caught sight of a longhaired blonde in the crowd. "She's going to have to make her way back toward the show ring. I'll take this side of the vendor tents and you take the other. We'll meet up at the other end. If you see anything, whistle."

Erin nodded and scurried away, peeking into the first tent as she went. I rushed to the other side, peering into each tent. No Claudine. Erin rounded the corner and shook her head. I pointed her toward the bathrooms and darted to the coat checks. We met up again outside the box office booth.

"Nothing," Erin said in answer to my questioning look.

We each took one side around the schooling ring. As I approached the far corner of the ring, an ear-splitting whistle ripped through the air and Erin motioned toward the VIP area.

There was Claudine, presenting her admission bracelet to the security guard and hobbling up to a front-row table.

Isabella Madderley trotted into the ring. Claudine

laughed at something one of her pampered friends wearing a red-and-white Yves St. Laurent lipstick dress whispered. She hung her cane by its silver handle from the top of the boards, not paying attention to Isabella's round.

Isabella finished with no faults and a better time of 41.98. The crowd's applause deafened.

I tried to push my way into the reserved area as if I belonged there. A security guard pulled me back by the arm. "Miss, this is a reserved area. You can't go in there."

The irony was that my parents had bought a table and I had every right to be there. But not Ally. Ally with her dirty jeans and slobber-smeared T-shirt belonged on this side of the fence.

"I'm Alexa Cheltingham," I said, with every bit of Cheltingham stiff-upper lip I could manage. Magnus's life was worth more than my cover. "My parents have a table."

He glared at me. "Your security bracelet says otherwise."

"This is important."

"I'm sure it is." He jerked his chin toward the exit. "Leave or I'll cuff you."

"See that blonde. Claudine Breitbach. She's going to try to hurt the next horse."

"Oh, yeah, how's she going to do that?"

With a gun? No, that didn't seem likely. Getting caught would defeat her purpose.

Drugs?

That ploy had worked successfully in the past when she played Horse Ripper to help Roman's chances along.

But Ross or I had been with Magnus night and day. Claudine had no opportunity to slip him anything before the class.

What else? It didn't matter. I had to distract her until Ross was finished with his round. I'd sit on her, if I had to.

"Listen," I told the guard, pushing forward. "This is a matter of life and death."

"Yeah, that's what they all say."

The announcer called Ross's name. My pulse took off at a mad gallop. I had to get in there. I had to stop Claudine.

Claudine gestured widely at her table companions and knocked her cane off the boards. She picked it up and placed it so the tip leaned against the top of the boards and the silver head pressed into her lap.

That's when I noticed the cane wasn't the wood one she'd leaned on this morning. In the glare of the arena lights, it reflected like metal. A barrel. A gun barrel. And Magnus would have to go by her on the first half of the combination that made up the second to last fence of this speed round.

She was going to shoot him and she already had her weapon trained. Was she crazy? How did she think she could get away with it?

I shoved my weight against the guard one more time. "This'll take less than a minute."

"That's it." He reached for the handcuffs at his belt. "Save it for the police."

"Sorry." I brushed behind him as if I intended to leave and whipped my arms around his throat in a chokehold. I really hated doing this, but he left me no choice. He scratched at my arms, but I squeezed until he passed out and slipped him into the chair by the entrance, leaving him slumped as if he were napping.

The starter gonged, and Ross and Magnus cantered to the first fence.

I rammed through the gate to the VIP seating. Claudine pointed the tip of her cane at Magnus.

"What's she doing here?"

"Hey, you're blocking the view."

I pounced on Claudine, bringing her down out of view so Magnus wouldn't spook. Her companions shrieked. She whipped the end of her cane around to club me. The metal tip struck my already bruised cheek and cut it open. The sting made me gasp and Claudine used my moment of weakness to roll over me and jump to her feet.

As she started to leave, I grabbed the end of the cane and yanked, pulling her off balance. She fell forward on top of me. Horrified gasps bloomed around us. I rolled over her. We crashed against a table leg, launching silver, china and crystal all around us.

I grappled to hold Claudine down while her stri-

dent companions in Manolo heels pulled at my
T-shirt with their acrylic nails. "Help! Security!"

More people joined the fray, trying to pry us apart.

"Well, really," someone said.

"What's going on?"

"They let all sorts of riff-raff in these days and
that's what it gets you."

The even rhythm of Magnus's hooves cantered
closer.

Claudine managed to raise herself to her knees
while strong male arms tugged me off her.

"She has a gun," I said. "The cane. Stop her!"

Ross cleared the fourth fence and turned at the end
of the area and headed straight toward us down the
last line.

She pointed her gun cane at Ross as he steered
Magnus toward the first fence of the combination.
Eyes cold and calculating, she pressed on the silver
head. A puff of air discharged.

I jerked my workout leg up and took the missile
full bore in the artificial shin.

Someone screamed, "Gun!"

People all around me flattened.

The bullet didn't leave a hole; it hung from the
denim of my jeans—a silver body with a black-tufted
tail. A dart. Tranquilizer? For once my prosthesis
was a blessing.

Ross cleared the vertical and gathered Magnus
for the second half of the combination.

I smiled at Claudine. "You lose."

She smiled back, a crooked thing filled with pure hatred and smacked her cane against the boards, creating an explosion of sound just as Magnus was taking off.

I broke through the hold imprisoning my arms and brought the witch down.

Magnus spooked and plowed through the fence, sending poles flying in all directions. The crowd gasped.

I wrenched the cane away from Claudine and rammed it into her collarbone, pinning her to the ground. She shrieked and tried to buck me off, but I rolled the cane to the base of her throat and pressed until her eyes bulged and she started to choke. I wasn't feeling the least bit charitable. "I told you not to mess with me."

Blood dripped from my cheek onto Claudine's silk dress. Ross would have had a clean round, if it weren't for her. After all Magnus had gone through, Ross deserved his perfect moment.

At least he'd stayed in the saddle. Magnus sailed over the last fence and sped through the finish line.

"Where are the cops?" I shouted, not sure how much longer I could hold Claudine. "This woman just tried to kill Ross Hardel."

The VIP area buzzed louder than a hive at swarming time. But even over the noise, I heard my mother's distinctive voice.

"Alexa? Is that you?"

I swore under my breath. Figures her inappropriate-behavior radar would go off.

Fortunately the cops arrived and hauled me and Claudine off to the station for questioning before Mom got her hands on me. I ended up in a small room whose air was tainted with the remnant of other people's fears.

The same detective who'd investigated Dawn's death plopped the cane and two plastic evidence bags on the table. One contained the dart I'd plucked out of my leg. The second my fake ID, which they'd confiscated as I tried to tell them who I was.

"Would you care to explain what happened this afternoon?" he asked.

I dabbed at the dried blood clotting my cut with a damp paper towel one of the cops had given me. "It's not too complicated. Claudine was shooting at Magnus and I stopped her. I'm pretty sure she's the Horse Ripper, not Karen Kallio."

"How'd you figure that out?"

I told him about the conversation I'd heard between Roman and Claudine and what'd I'd learned about Claudine's money problems from the other grooms. "I followed my hunch. Maybe Claudine thought that if she helped Roman win, he'd marry her." I figured that was all the cops needed to know at this point.

"Just a hunch, huh?" The detective scratched his head as if he was confused. "Would you care to tell me why you were using a fake name and working as a groom at the Ashcroft Equestrian Center? Don't bother suggesting you needed some extra cash."

I swallowed a sigh of frustration. "I've already told you. I was protecting the horses."

"That's some coincidence how you just happened to start working the same week the Horse Ripper showed up at the very same stable."

I gritted my teeth to hold in my temper so this ordeal could end. "It wasn't a coincidence. I had a feeling the Horse Ripper would target the equestrian center."

"Oh, I get it, another one of your hunches. How come one little girl like you could figure this Horse Ripper thing when three police departments and the FBI were baffled?"

"You were looking from the outside in and not getting anywhere. Horses were dying. So I decided to look from the inside out."

He scratched his jaw. "All on your own?"

I wasn't about to tell him the part about working undercover for the Gotham Rose Club. There was no point putting the whole agency or anyone I loved in jeopardy just because I'd failed as an agent.

"I told you. I love horses. Since my accident, horses have been a symbol of hope for me—as they are to my foundation's clients. I couldn't stand the thought of someone preying on innocent animals." My fingers scratched at the edge of my socket as I explained Hardel Industries' secret project. "When I realized how much was at stake with Magnus showing, I couldn't believe that Karen Kallio was the Horse Ripper—"

"Another hunch?"

"Whatever," I said obstinately. "But I knew the real target was Magnus and Ross's project." And although I'd failed at being a Gotham Rose agent, I hadn't failed my foundation's clients who might soon benefit from Ross's project. I'd stopped Claudine from cheating them out of their hope.

The detective stared at me, plainly skeptical. I braced myself for a bumpy ride. His forehead crimped and he poked at the bag containing my Ally Cross ID. "So you just up and got yourself some fake ID and hired yourself off as a groom. Tell me again where you got this ID?"

"The Internet. You'd be amazed what you can buy on eBay."

"Are you aware there's a severe penalty for misrepresenting yourself to a police officer—especially in a murder investigation?"

I stifled a sigh. My mother was going to disown me if the police pressed charges against me. I just wanted to go home, soak my bruises in my spa tub, put on clean clothes and sleep for a week. "I guess I'll have to get a lawyer."

With those magic words, a knock sounded on the door. "Miss Cheltingham's parents are insisting on seeing their daughter."

Great, let the drama begin. My mother elbowed her way into the room and clutched at her chest when she saw me. "Alexa! Do you know how embarrassed I was to realize that the unkempt stablehand engaged in a fist fight was my own daughter?"

I dropped the paper towel on the table, so she could see me in my full glory of filth, sweat and bruises. "Frankly, everything I do is an embarrassment to you. And you know what? I'm not going to waste another second trying to please you."

"Alexa, how dare you speak to your own mother that way—" She gasped. "That cut is going to need a plastic surgeon!"

As if preventing a scar was the most important thing right now. "It's no big deal, Mom."

Fortunately my father intervened before a full-blown family argument erupted. "Jacquelyn, we'll sort this out at home." He turned to the detective. "Are we done here? My daughter has had a rough day and she needs medical treatment."

"We're just trying to figure it all out, Mr. Cheltingham," the detective said.

"In the meantime, she's done what you couldn't do. She's caught your Horse Ripper."

"We'll be wanting to talk to you again, Ms. Cheltingham."

"Contact us through our lawyer," my father said firmly and led me away.

Once they got me away from the interrogation

room, my father lit into me. "How could you go and do something idiotic as playing Jane Bond? You could have been killed!"

"I was never in any danger, Daddy. Claudine was after horses, not humans."

"You could have been killed."

The look of pure panic in his eyes told me he was having flashbacks to my accident ten years ago when he'd arrived at school to find me in a pool of blood. I wrapped one arm around his waist and hugged him tight. "I'm sorry I scared you, but I'm all grown-up now."

I was no longer that fifteen-year-old angry at the world for cheating her out of a life. I could make my own way. And the knowledge that I was strong enough to live with the consequences buoyed me. What were a few police questions compared to Magnus's safety? And the integrity of Ross's project? All in all the outcome was good, even though I'd blown my chance to work for the Gotham Rose Club. I could still do a lot of good through my foundation.

A buzzing noise on the other side of the front doors stopped us. I couldn't go out there. My cover was blown, and paparazzi swarmed outside the station like larvae on a kill. The reporters expected an explanation as to why Alexa Cheltingham was dressed as a groom, but the only person I wanted to see was Ross.

I played into my mother's sense of propriety by

dusting my dirty jeans and patting my disheveled bun. "I can't go out there looking like this."

"No, you most certainly cannot," my mother said in a tone so pinched I found my posture straightening automatically.

"You go out front and handle the sensation stalkers, and I'll slip out the back. I'll meet you at home."

My mother nodded, putting on her most regal air. "That sounds like the first intelligent plan you've had all day."

I ducked out a back door and wound my way to the showgrounds. Getting my cut fixed could wait. The uppermost thought on my mind was finding Ross before he saw the evening news.

I found Ross with Magnus, and the sight of him so gentle with the horse nearly undid my courage. We'd been lying to each other for over a week. At least one truth would come out today.

I took a deep breath. Longshot, and relative newcomer on the circuit, Isabella Madderley, had won the Grand Prix. After Magnus's rounds, the jumps were reset and Roman got his moment in the spotlight. But he choked and couldn't ride Trademark fast enough to beat Isabella. The faults Magnus incurred because of Claudine put Ross in third place.

"I'm so sorry," I said to Ross as he wrapped shipping boots around Magnus's legs. My nerves jumped as if I was about to enter the ring for the most important show of my life. And maybe, in a way, I was.

"I expected to see you after my round," Ross said.

"I ended up at the police station, giving a statement about Claudine's trying to shoot Magnus."

"I owe you once more. Thanks for saving Magnus."

I crossed my arms over my chest. "Don't you mean Indigo Flash?

He eyed me thoughtfully. "How long have you known?"

I shrugged. "I saw you dye him one night and that revved up my curiosity. So I borrowed one of your company's ID scanners and put one and one together. I couldn't let anyone get to him. Not after he'd been hurt so badly—and your project could benefit so many people." I stroked Magnus's muzzle and his mobile lips searched for a sugar cube. "I'm just sorry he didn't win."

"Ah, but we lost spectacularly," Ross said with surprising cheerfulness for someone who'd just lost a major competition. "Anyone can knock down a rail. It takes talent to demolish a whole jump and still make the next."

"You and he deserved to win."

His smile widened, creasing his cheeks. "This wasn't about ribbons or cups or prizes. This was about Magnus. And *he* won big. Three years ago he could barely walk. And today he was in the final round at a major Grand Prix."

Ross grabbed me and twirled me around. His joy was so infectious that my blood started to sing. He put me down, his big hands resting on my waist, eagerness playing wickedly in his eyes. "Come to the ball with me tonight. I have a big announcement to make, and after all you've done to protect Magnus, it seems only right that you're there."

"I can't go with you, Ross." My job was done. I just wanted to go home and soak in my marble tub. "Since we're being honest, you should know that my name isn't Ally Cross."

A smile unfurled and rippled with laughter. "Say yes, Alexa. Come to the ball with me. I need you there."

Ross had said Alexa, not Ally. I gasped, searching through his face. "You knew?"

"You think I'd forget that sassy ass of yours? Not after following it in boring dressage lesson after boring dressage lesson." His eyes gleamed with mischief. "Gave me something interesting to focus on."

"When did you figure out who I was?"

"As soon as you blew by me on Bandit that day."

My bottom had given me away, not my leg. How was that for irony? Then I punched him on the shoulder. "You knew and you tortured me by telling me how much you hated Alexa Cheltingham?"

"I wanted to see you squirm." He rubbed his shoulder. "Besides, for a while I thought you were there to steal my business secrets."

"Never. This was always about the horses." At least that much was the truth.

His brow furrowed. "I can't figure out why you'd do this at all. Playing a groom is something I never pictured you doing."

"Shows how little you know about me." I really didn't have a good explanation, but I needed to tell him something, so I couched the lie in truth. "Belinda is a friend and she was worried about the Horse Ripper. She wasn't planning on riding this summer because of the baby, but she and Patrick Dunhill are good friends. So when one of his grooms was fired, Belinda suggested I'd be willing to keep an eye out for the Horse Ripper."

"Why?"

"Because I know horses, and Patrick and Belinda both knew they could trust me."

That trust word hung between us again.

"I'm not sure I believe you."

My ears flamed incinerator hot. "You haven't from Day One, so I'm not expecting a magical change of attitude. Go ahead and think what you want."

I whirled around, but he caught my elbow and pulled me back to him. "Is your temper always on such a trigger switch?"

"Only when things matter," slipped out before I could stop it.

"Yeah? So I matter?"

Yes. "No, of course not."

He laced his fingers through mine and further scrambled my thought circuits with a torrid kiss that said he had all the time in the world and was going to take it. I was melting again and I didn't really want to stop. I sighed when he gently kissed the cut on my cheek and pulled back. "Tell me again I don't matter."

"Maybe a little."

He tucked a loose strand of my hair behind my ear. "I heard about your accident ten years ago."

I wasn't ready to talk about that minefield any more than he was ready to talk about how his mother died or what was really going on between him and Roman. "As you see I survived."

"You did more than that." His gaze took on that blue laser quality that tended to make me melt. "Be my date tonight, Alexa."

I wavered. Ally Cross had done her job. The time had come to drop my alter ego and slip back into my own skin. I might as well take that first step tonight. I needed to talk to Renee anyway and she'd be at the ball.

"I thought you couldn't stand the thought of spending an evening with Alexa Cheltingham."

"She grows on you."

Chapter 15

Once the horses were on their way home, I unabashedly brandished my mother's name to get our family doctor to stitch my cut. What was the point of pull if you didn't use it? And this was for a good cause. Mom would understand. She would not, however, understand that I hadn't dropped by the penthouse for the little chat they expected. I took the chicken's way out and left a message that I was detained at the doctor's office and that I'd see her and dad at the ball. Ross's announcement tonight would usher in a world of hope, and I wanted to look my best.

After a shower, I begged Kristi to come to my home and fix the damage she'd done. In an hour, she had my hair back to its regular deep mahogany and the curls under control and she'd managed to make my nails presentable.

I'd ditched the colored lenses and my own sienna eyes stared back at me from the mirror. Makeup took care of the scratches and bruises. As for the bandage covering the five stitches on my cheek, it was a small price to pay for Magnus's safety.

I slipped on a slinky Ralph Lauren dress that clung to all the right places. The silk heated under my fingers as I smoothed the skirt. Red. Sexy. I smiled as I imagined Ross's jaw dropping when he saw me. Alexa Cheltingham was definitely not as boring as he thought. I twirled in front of the full-length mirror. Perfect.

From one of the cubbyholes in the walk-in closet of my Park Avenue penthouse bedroom, I plucked a Judith Leiber satin-and-crystal handbag that complemented the dress. To the lipstick, keys and half a photograph I'd dropped in my bag, I was just about to add the Tiffany cigarette case that had followed me wherever I went since I'd gotten out of the hospital ten years ago.

I sat on the vanity stool. The silver was cold in my palm. I opened the clasp and stared at the half-burnt symbol of my dreams gone up in smoke. But Ally had shown me that I didn't need to prove myself to anyone. To live my life fully was the best gift I could give myself, and I intended to take it.

I closed the case and threw it in the garbage.

With a last check at my makeup, I snapped off the light and went down to the lobby to meet Ross.

The final event of the Metropolitan Spring Classic Charity Horse Show was held in a glass ballroom at the top of a downtown hotel and was already in full swing by the time we arrived.

Ross, impeccable in his Hugo Boss tux, immediately swept me onto the dance floor.

Renee was there, dancing with her husband, Preston, newly released from prison. She glowed in a blue Gucci dress with a twist at the bodice. The royal blue matched that of her eyes. So did the sapphires at her ears. Preston looked a little pale, but otherwise smart in his tuxedo and bow tie. I also spotted Olivia Hayworth, Renee's assistant, and several of the Gotham Rose agents.

At the height of the ball, Ross stepped onto the stage. "As most of you know, Hardel Industries has been working on a revolutionary project for a decade. The purchase of VetTech allowed us to combine nanobiotechnology with the sensoceutical research that VetTech had already undertaken and produced a miracle."

Pride and passion spun off him into a brilliant halo. He cued the AV technician, and the film of Indigo Flash's accident three years ago played in life-size color on a screen behind him. The crowd gasped. "I won't bore you with all the technical details, but the short story is that after that fall, Indigo Flash no longer had full use of his hind legs."

He cued the technician one more time. Magnus's first round in this afternoon's Grand Prix class filled the screen. "This is Indigo Flash today. Our new technology has allowed us to insert a nanochip that has helped to do something thought impossible. The chip implanted in Indigo's spine, with the help of the sensoceuticals, has regenerated nerves and redirected their growth."

A hubbub rippled through the crowd. I clapped and cheered. Now that the secret was out, Magnus was safe.

Renee caught my attention and signaled me to join her near the main entrance to the ballroom. I plucked a flute of champagne from a passing waiter. Renee seemed uneasy and distracted as I approached. Was something wrong? Or had my request to speak to her tonight made her uncomfortable now that I was no longer an agent?

By tacit agreement, we went out to a private alcove so we wouldn't be overheard. The drone of music played on, muffled by the closed ballroom doors.

"I don't think Dawn's murder is related to the Horse Ripper, but it's definitely related to Magnus. But Magnus should be safe now that his secret is out in the open."

"Yes, you're right. Ross kept his secret well." She glanced around the hallway as if she expected a monster to jump out of the shadows.

"Renee? Are you all right?"

Her smile was thin and tight. "I'm fine. You did a good job, Alexa. I'm really proud of you. I hope you're planning on staying with us."

"You mean I'm not out?"

She looked at me for the first time. "Whatever gave you that idea?"

"You pulled me off the case and I kept investigating solo."

She turned back to the hallway as if she were looking for someone specific. "I should have trusted your instincts. You were on the scene, and we were looking at the data from the outside. What's important is that the Horse Ripper is in jail and the technology is in safe hands. Karen will be released in the morning."

I opened my bag and retrieved the half photograph of Dawn's that had puzzled me. "I found this in Dawn's things. I think she might have been using it to blackmail the man in the other half of the photograph. And I think whoever he is, he's the one who wanted to steal the technology."

Renee took the sliver of photo from me and stared at the woman and child. As she turned the picture over, her hand shook. Her face turned whiter than the platinum chain at her neck.

Before I could say anything, she excused herself and hurried away.

I was right. The picture had meaning.

Alan wandered out into the hallway, dapper as usual. He held a flute of champagne and a plate of desserts. "You look lovely tonight, darling."

"You look hot yourself."

"That was great footage of you choking Claudine Breitbach with a cane. Stylish. The tongues are wagging like crazy."

I twirled the silk cord of my bag. "I did what I had to do."

He chewed on a small éclair. "What's next for you, darling?"

I needed to get away from the city, from everything familiar while I sorted out what I wanted to do and how I wanted to do it. I was too confused, especially about Ross, to think straight. Prague sounded far enough and foreign enough to fit the bill. "Nat's whisking me off to another film festival next weekend."

Gaze fixed somewhere over my shoulder, Alan smiled wickedly. "Oh, I think you'll get a better offer."

"Who was that?" Ross asked, cupping a palm around my elbow.

"An old friend." Someone bumped into me, pushing me closer to Ross.

"Good. I hate competition." The kiss he planted at the base of my neck reverberated all the way down to my toes. "I'd like to see more of you."

"Why?" I fiddled with my empty champagne flute. "I mean—"

Amusement warbled through his voice. "I'll answer the why. Because you're a woman of courage. You're not afraid of hard work. You didn't mind getting down and dirty to protect a horse. Or putting one of your own in jail."

He took my hand. "Dance with me?"

My mouth went dry. There was something important I needed to get out of the way first. "There's something I want to show you."

During the ten-minute car ride to my apartment, unease coiled with every turn of the tires, with every beep of horn. Was I crazy to take Ross home? I tried to speak, but my throat was too dry, my thoughts too jumbled. He looked at me with curiosity, but kept his questions to himself as he rubbed the back of my hand with a thumb in a slow, soothing rhythm.

I led him through the length of my apartment with its Mediterranean spa decor and onto the balcony where the bright city lights played against the dark canvas of night like a laser show.

"Ross?" I turned my back to the wide cityscape and faced him. My insides twisted into a knot. I liked him. Too much. Enough to take a chance.

"What?" He leaned against the door frame watching me patiently.

I sat down on one of the upholstered deck chairs that flanked the tall window. Without a word, I pushed aside the long slit on the right side of the dress's skirt. I rolled down the cuff of my pretty leg off the residual limb and propped the prosthesis on the wall beside me.

My cheeks grew hot. I wiped my hands restlessly on my silk-covered thighs.

Ross crouched in front of me and reached out to trace the red scar with the tips of his fingers. His touch was firm and tender. Not afraid. A flutter quickened my heart, spreading a feeling I couldn't quite place. And when he looked up from the scarred flesh that ended below my knee, my vision blurred. It was as though I was finding firm footing for the first time.

Right now, right here, I was all that I could be and it was enough.

Ross took hold of my chin and forced me to look at him. "Is that supposed to scare me off?"

"I hope not." I'd just bet my heart that he could look at my missing leg and still like what he saw. And then I was scared again because the root of contentment had run so deep, so fast. There was no going back to hiding behind the person I'd once been. "It does most people."

"I'm not most people. You should know that by now."

His eyes were true blue. True enough to have seen beyond a broken horse into the realm of possibilities. And in that true blue, I now saw the reflection of that wide-open acceptance for me.

"I liked you ten years ago," he said.

"Oh, yeah, then how come it was Kati Coates you chased and kissed?" I asked unconvinced.

"Kati was easy. I didn't have the experience to handle someone like you."

I frowned. "What's that supposed to mean?"

"Women like you are for the long haul." My expression must have shown puzzlement because he added, "For when a guy gets serious."

He wanted to get serious? With me?

Then a grin split his face, deepening his dimples. "Besides, Roman's the leg man." He rose, pulling me onto my one good leg, and palmed my bottom with both hands, balancing me. "I've always been an ass man. Yours looks particularly good in this dress."

He held me tight in his arms and kissed me without my prosthesis on. His heartbeat met mine in a perfect song that made me forget all about my handicap.

He swerved his lips to my ear and in a gruff voice said, "So about seeing more of you?"

I wound my arms around his neck, dug my fingers into his hair and nipped at his earlobe with my teeth. "I'd say there's a better-than-average chance of that happening." I was more than ready for the next step. "Let's go inside."

The following item appeared in Rubi Cho's "In the Know" column the next morning:

"Claudine Breitbach, sports heiress, was a real showstopper at yesterday's show-jumping Grand Prix with her dart-loaded cane. She tried to kill her lover's competition. Said competition just happens to be lover boy's own twin brother. Following a public tussle with an heiress, who we all know has a soft spot for horses, Ms. B. was arrested on charges of killing the eight horses attributed to the Horse Ripper—both in Connecticut and in Palm Beach. More charges are likely to follow. If convicted, Ms. B.'s next residence could be a nice twelve-by-fourteen cell, à la Martha Stewart.

"In other news, a little birdie told me, there's one girl with a leg up on the competition when it comes to winning R.H.'s attention. Stay tuned. More to come."

* * * * *

A Model Spy

by

Natalie Dunbar

In the quiet sanctuary of her office, Renee secured the door, slipped into her powder room and locked that door too. Making herself comfortable on the overstuffed white loveseat, she lifted the receiver from the vanity table. "This is Renee Dalton Sinclair."

"Renee… I trust you're enjoying Pres's return?" the mechanically distorted voice began.

Renee was overjoyed to have her husband back, but the sound of his name in the disembodied voice sent chills through her. Was there a threat lurking beneath the Governess's question?

"I love my husband," she answered simply, her tone ringing with strength and conviction. "Having him home has brought the life back to our house." In the ensuing silence she added, "Of course, I'm grateful for anything you've done to obtain his early release."

"Preston Sinclair was innocent," the Governess replied smugly. "Let's move on to the business at hand. Have you seen the story in the papers about the two models who were killed in their Miami apartments? Another model was caught at Miami International yesterday, trying to smuggle heroin into the city in a case of bubble bath."

"I saw the stories," Renee confirmed. "You'd think that fashion models would have more options than the poor desperate souls who normally end up being mules in the drug trade."

The Governess expelled a contemptuous puff of air. "Someone made those models an offer they couldn't refuse. There's an active drug gang operating in New York and Miami and they're targeting models for mules. We need to identify this gang, find out who's at the top, get the evidence, and take them down fast."

Shifting the phone and its cord, Renee used her key to open a drawer at the carved antique vanity and remove the large file containing pictures and press information on all the Gotham Roses. Some of the women were merely members of her charitable organization that required all its members to pay twenty-five thousand dollars to join, ten thousand a year afterward, and then asked that they help raise at least one hundred thousand dollars a year.

She knew by heart which members were also a part of her undercover organization. They were the best, the brightest and most capable women imaginable. "We need someone who can move in the modeling and music worlds without raising suspicion," she murmured, paging past several members. "Someone they would actually welcome."

"We also need a high profile, well-connected operative who can take care of herself. Vanessa Dawson would be ideal," the Governess said in a firm voice. "We've arranged for her to get a contract with Inside Sports magazine for the Fantasy Swimsuit edition."

Finding Vanessa's gorgeous picture and press information in the stack, Renee shook her head. "Vanessa left the modeling world under less than ideal circumstances," she began. "It would take a lot to get her back into that life."

"The stakes are high," the Governess insisted. "Lives have been lost. The murdered models moved in circles that included some of the younger members of the old money set. What if there is a connection between their money and the models acting as mules for the drug trade?"

What if, indeed. As an heiress and bone fide member of the old money set, Renee knew bored people with more money than they knew what to do with were liable to do anything.

Renee closed her file, already imaging Vanessa back into the wild, unpredictable world she'd barely escape. She knew Vanessa could successful complete the assignment…but at what cost?

♥ SILHOUETTE®
Sensation™

FEELS LIKE HOME
by Maggie Shayne

When Chicago cop Jimmy Corona returned to his small hometown, all he wanted was to find a mother to care for his son while he did his job. Shy, kind-hearted, Kara Brand was the obvious choice. But danger soon followed Jimmy, and only Kara stood between his son and certain death…

THE SHERIFF OF HEARTBREAK COUNTY
by Kathleen Creighton

A congressman's son is murdered and everything points to Mary Owen, the newcomer to Hartsville… but Sheriff Roan Harley can't quite make the pieces fit. At first his interest in Mary is purely because of the investigation. But where will his loyalties lie when he realises he's in love?

WARRIOR WITHOUT RULES
by Nancy Gideon

Bodyguard Zach Russell was charged with protecting risk-taking heiress Antonia Catillo, but his weakness for the beauty was getting in the way. Threats on Antonia's life were growing serious as their long-suppressed attraction rose to the surface. Could Zach crack the case before it was too late?

On sale from 17th November 2006

Available at WHSmith, Tesco, ASDA, Borders, Eason,
Sainsbury's and most bookshops

www.silhouette.co.uk

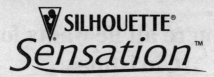
EXCLUSIVE by Katherine Garbera

Bombshell – Athena Force

Investigative reporting was Tory Patton's calling, and when her fellow Athena Academy graduate was taken hostage, nothing would stop her from taking the assignment to save her friend. But the kidnappers weren't who they seemed… and suddenly this crisis came much closer to the academy than anyone could ever guess.

THE BEAST WITHIN by Suzanne McMinn

PAX

The thing Keiran Holt feared most lived inside him—and possibly could cause harm to the woman he'd married. But Paige wasn't the only one who had spent two years looking for her missing husband. Would he be captured before they could save their once passionate marriage…and tame the beast within?

MODEL SPY by Natalie Dunbar

Bombshell –The IT Girls

A former supermodel from a wealthy family, Vanessa Dawson was perfect for the Gotham Roses' latest mission: Two top models were dead and it seemed a drug-ring was operating from the highest level of the fashion industry. Vanessa went undercover to get to the truth, but soon shoot-outs replaced fashion shoots as the order of the day…

On sale from 17th November 2006

FREE

4 BOOKS AND A SURPRISE GIFT!

We would like to take this opportunity to thank you for reading this Silhouette® book by offering you the chance to take FOUR more specially selected titles from the Sensation™ series absolutely FREE! We're also making this offer to introduce you to the benefits of the Mills & Boon® Reader Service™—

- ★ **FREE home delivery**
- ★ **FREE gifts and competitions**
- ★ **FREE monthly Newsletter**
- ★ **Books available before they're in the shops**
- ★ **Exclusive Reader Service offers**

Accepting these FREE books and gift places you under no obligation to buy; you may cancel at any time, even after receiving your free shipment. Simply complete your details below and return the entire page to the address below. You don't even need a stamp!

YES! Please send me 4 free Sensation books and a surprise gift. I understand that unless you hear from me, I will receive 6 superb new titles every month for just £3.10 each, postage and packing free. I am under no obligation to purchase any books and may cancel my subscription at any time. The free books and gift will be mine to keep in any case.

S6ZEE

Ms/Mrs/Miss/Mr..........................Initials ....
BLOCK CAPITALS PLEASE

Surname ....

Address ....

....

....Postcode ....

Send this whole page to:
The Reader Service, FREEPOST CN81, Croydon, CR9 3WZ